SHADOWS REMAIN

A novella

TIM McWHORTER

Cover Design by Tim McWhorter
Cover Photo by Kathy Gold
Edited by Ryan McDaniel

Second Edition

Author's Note

When I originally turned out this novella, it was simply a test to see if I could, having only written short stories up to that point. Subsequently, it was only published with the thought of sharing it with family and friends. The idea of anyone else purchasing the little book never entered my mind. So when that started happening, (shipping all over the globe, no less) I was equal parts ecstatic and concerned. While I liked the story a great deal and felt it was a solid read, I also knew that it wasn't as good as it could be. Spending more time and money on the cover than the editing is a well-known rookie mistake. And I made it. A point repeatedly stated in the reviews. While most liked the book, several readers pointed out the need for further editing.

As time went on and I started building a catalogue of books, (something else I'd never dreamed of) increasingly more readers were being turned onto *Shadows Remain*. Naturally, the idea of pulling the book from shelves and giving it a makeover started entering my thoughts. At the end of 2016, I did just that. And while taking the book out of print made me a little sad, I focused more on its future and less on past nostalgia. Now, after several months, this book you're holding stands on its own. Not to mention, it's now one that I can stand proudly behind.

If you already own a first edition copy of *Shadows Remain*, awesome. I appreciate that you've given this second edition a look. If, however, this is your first foray into the shadows, I hope you like what you find here. Just remember…

"Life itself is but the shadow of death, and souls departed but the shadows of the living." – Sir Thomas Browne

Other Titles by Tim McWhorter

Bone White

Blackened

Swallowing the Worm and Other Short Stories

The Winding Down Hours (Autumn 2017)

September 17, 1987

The scream was high and shrill, full of fear and lacking any sense of hope. It came from all directions, echoing off the granite headstones, filling the air like thick pollen. A scream like I'd never heard, yet there was a certain familiarity to it. Something I recognized. Not its tone, but its source.

"Connor!" My shout paled in comparison to the wail of anguish assaulting my ears from the darkness.

"Come on, Adam!" Nick pulled at my red and black flannel sleeve, ripping it at the shoulder. "We gotta get outta here, man! We gotta go!"

When our eyes met, the moonlight turned his damp eyes to glass; fear pried them wide.

"We can't just leave him!" I pleaded. "We can't leave Connor!"

We stood at the entrance to the only cemetery in Broken Tree, our youthful courage expired. Nick was already through the towering iron gate, imploring me to join him from the perceived safety beyond the fence. But my feet wouldn't move. My hands wouldn't free the iron bars clutched tightly in my white-knuckled fists. I was frozen. Frozen with fear. Frozen with the realization that our game of hide and seek had suddenly taken a wrong turn.

A very wrong turn.

"Connor!" I yelled my friend's name one last time before

slipping through the gate and joining Nick on the other side. The screams had died away, and other than the rhythmic drumming of my heart in my ears, the echo of my voice was the only sound cutting through the silence.

It took another hard wrench of my arm to break the cemetery's pull.

Then I ran. Finally, I ran.

We'd left our bicycles propped against a tree only twenty yards from the gate, yet it took forever to reach them. Working the pedals like our lives depended on it, we sped down the country road and into our neighborhood, weaving through streets, sidewalks and the occasional side yard on our way to the intersection of Locust and Willow. We knew the route by heart, and the moonlight made our navigation easier, despite the lack of streetlamps in our neighborhood.

Toward homes with darkened windows and sleeping parents, clueless of our midnight antics in the graveyard, we pedaled as fast as our twelve-year-old legs could work. It wasn't the first time the three of us had played in the cemetery at night, but I had the unsettling feeling it would be the last. Three friends, who'd played together, grown up together, and as of last week, had lost our innocence together by way of the stack of dirty magazines we'd discovered in a dumpster.

But that's where the togetherness would end. Of the three of us, only two were leaving the graveyard.

"He'll make it home." Nick didn't lack for optimism as we stood on the corner of Willow and Locust, straddling our bikes, taking a moment to catch our breaths. Risking the occasional glance behind us, we made sure we weren't being followed. I wasn't sure what might be following, or what we would do about it, but that's what made the whole thing even more frightening.

"He'll be knockin' on our doors in the morning," Nick said. "You'll see."

I looked at him with his long, dark hair hanging over his eyes. Did he really believe that? But, I didn't question my friend's confidence out loud. In fact, I didn't say a word as Nick turned up Willow without so much as a wave and started peddling the two-block trek to his house. After a final glance back in the direction of the cemetery, I walked my bike across the street to my own house and headed around the side and into the shadows where my bedroom window waited.

Moments later, I crawled under the new Superman sheets my mother had recently bought me. I'd slept over at Connor's a couple of weeks before and came home talking nonstop about his Green Lantern sheets that glowed in the dark. Even though my Superman sheets didn't glow in the dark, I was happy with mine. Superman was the man of steel. Able to leap tall buildings. Stop trains and bullets and all manner of bad intentions. Right now, though, all I wanted was to be protected from a boogeyman who had just proven his existence to our group of three, just in case we had ever doubted.

I pulled the sheets and comforter up over my head, focused on the ticking of the alarm clock sitting on my dresser; anything to block out the scream reverberating inside my skull.

Tick...tock...tick...

It didn't help.

*   *   *

The following morning brought a knock on the door, but it wasn't Connor, and somehow I knew it wouldn't be. It was a police officer. I watched from the top of the stairs, an unsettled feeling in the pit of my stomach as he entered the house and shook my dad's hand. The shiny gold badge pinned to his chest was the first thing I noticed, standing out against the dark blue of his uniform. But my focus soon turned to the officer's hat. I thought it was strange that he wasn't wearing his hat, but simply had it tucked under his arm. Did that mean something?

I strained to hear the conversation, but the words were hushed, and I couldn't make out many. Their voices ascended the stairs in a soft murmur, interrupted a moment later by a wail of anguish from my mother. I didn't have to wait long to find out what the visit was about. Only minutes after escorting the officer into the front room, my father emerged at the bottom of the stairs, calling for me to come down. The expression on his face ensured me that the unsettled feeling in my stomach was indeed warranted.

"Adam, this is Officer Wilson."

I scanned the room for my mother, but she must have left because her's wasn't among the concerned faces. After being instructed to have a seat on our brown plaid couch, I was told that Officer Wilson had a few questions for me. I was also told that I wouldn't get into trouble over any of my answers. But that doesn't do much to calm a young boy's nerves when a policeman is standing in his parent's living room with a list of questions for him. My nervousness must have been obvious, because I was told to relax.

Ten minutes later, the officer flipped his notebook shut, rose from the couch with a reassuring smile and told my dad he'd be in touch. After he escorted the officer out, it was my dad's turn to ask me some questions before finally, with a gentle hand on my knee, explaining the situation: around the same time Connor's mother was finding his bed empty that morning, a grounds worker for the cemetery was making a discovery of his own. While mowing the grass, he'd come across a small red sneaker outside the abandoned receiving vault. Taking a look inside, he found Connor's body.

My father had spared me the gruesome details, but later that morning I'd heard my parents discussing them in the kitchen. Conner had been nearly naked, slumped against the back wall of the vault surrounded by a couple of thread-bare blankets, tin cans and a trash bag stuffed with assorted clothing. He was alone and covered in mud and blood, only his ripped t-shirt, socks and one shoe remained of Connor's clothes. Even his glasses were missing. He'd been strangled and discarded, left lying on a pile of wilted flowers that had been tossed inside the vault to rot. He died alone, the cemetery's residents his only companions.

It was less than a week later that the transfer my father had been expecting came in. Within days, my parents were driving down Interstate 74, me in the backseat, and Broken Tree, Minnesota growing smaller in the rear-view mirror. We hadn't stayed long enough for me to officially mourn Connor with friends and classmates. And whether it was because of Connor Westphal's death or not, we never looked back.

Chapter One – Present Day

The cardboard boxes in the back of the moving truck were heavier than those in the front. At least that's how it seemed. Either that, or my thirty-six-year-old back was starting to protest the physical labor. All morning, the voice in my head spun a broken record, reminding me that all the hours sitting behind a drafting table and computer monitor were taking a toll. The twenty extra pounds I was carrying around my middle probably weren't helping, either. It was only eleven o'clock in the morning, and I was already in desperate need of a shower. The transformation of my t-shirt from light grey to dark was nearly complete, and my odiferous scent could best be described as "foul."

It had been a long morning spent carrying boxes, mattress springs, dining room chairs, office equipment, architectural supplies and everything else we'd brought with us on the eighteen-hundred-mile trip from Tucson. We'd rolled into town in the wee hours, caught a couple restless hours in sleeping bags spread out on our new living room floor, then cracked the lock on the U-Haul right around 7:00 am, coffee in hand. As the morning wore on, the only other thought besides the broken record regarding my sedentary life was: *I should've hired someone.*

"Sixteen!" Ben shouted, buzzing me on his bike the way Maverick buzzed the control tower in that movie I'd let him watch a couple weeks ago. He'd liked the movie so much that he watched it four more times over the weekend, much to his mother's distress. When she had caught him curled up on the couch with the volume down one night when he was supposed to be in bed sleeping, he wasn't the only one who caught hell for it.

Jumping out of Ben's way, I nearly dropped the box with the word "kitchen" scribbled across the top. It was roughly the size of a dog house, so luckily, I recovered just in time. As I checked my pant leg, making sure I hadn't dribbled on myself, I felt a hand on my arm.

"Careful there, Mr. Bishop."

"Oh, hey, Babe." Whether I needed it or not, my wife was the kind of woman who was always telling me to be careful, to watch out for things. Even that which was beyond my control. She apparently labored under the misconception that I was either a klutz or a child. Not that she was entirely wrong.

"I think this one's yours." I showed her the box I was holding. "It has your name on it."

Cheryl pulled the box down to her level, reading aloud the word she herself had written. "Really? Maybe it's time you familiarized yourself with the contents of that box. You're a big boy now. I think you could handle it."

That's when I screwed up and did something I really should have known better than to do. I chuckled. Actually, I full on guffawed. I couldn't help it. It simply came out. And as I knew it would, it only encouraged her.

"You know, there's really nothing in a kitchen that you should be afraid of." Her voice had taken on a condescending tone that only a mother possessed. "It's a wondrous room where magical things can happen. And I'm not just talking about cooking—"

Ben zipped passed on his red Huffy. "Seventeen!"

A gasp escaped Cheryl as she pulled herself into me, the close quarters making the box grow even heavier.

"What's he doing?" Cheryl asked, stepping back and giving me some room. One hand went to her chest, the other tucked strands of hair behind her ear.

"Well, Goose, the man says he has the need, the need for speed." It was a poor man's excuse for an impersonation, but I wasn't thinking of quitting my day job anytime soon. When she gave me the "I still don't think that movie was appropriate" look for the hundredth time, I chose to drop the *Top Gun* references. "He's taking laps. From the corner to the lamppost and back."

We watched Ben work the pedals like he was fleeing a zombie apocalypse. Once he reached the lamppost, he stood on the brake, leaving yet another long black streak to mar the concrete. When he looked back at us with a satisfied smile and waved, it was Cheryl's turn to look at me with a smile of her own. Then out of the blue, she hugged me. In order to bypass the box that I was pretty certain I was going to drop at any second, she had to come at me from the side.

"He's so gonna love it here, Adam." She'd placed her lips so close to my ear that her breathy words tickled. "I think this'll be good for him. A cramped apartment in the sweatiest city in the country is no place to raise a family."

Her dislike of Tucson ranked up there with eight-legged basement dwellers and boxed mac & cheese. The only reason she'd been drawn there in the first place was the nursing program at the University of Arizona. By the time she'd earned her degree, she'd met me and had fallen in love. She had been 'stuck' there ever since. Her words. As an up and comer at a respected architectural firm, I wouldn't be ready to leave for a few more years. Against her parent's wishes, she chose me over returning home to Philadelphia. Still, she never passed up an opportunity to remind me how much she hated the constant heat of Arizona. Dry or not.

"This'll be good for all of us," I said, desperate to be rid of the box of kitchenware. "Now, if you don't mind, I really need to put this box down before my arms tear from their joints and I drop all your stuff."

The hurt from the punch in the arm was a good hurt, and I told her so.

Chapter Two

The smoky aroma of bacon aroused me to the good news; it was Friday. Cheryl always got up a little earlier on Fridays to make a hot breakfast for Ben and me. It was equal parts celebration of the coming weekend, and welcome respite from the Pop-tarts and handfuls of cold cereal we grabbed on our way out the door the rest of the week. Cheryl despised breakfast herself, avoiding it the way some people avoid the dentist. She preferred to start her days with a pair of skinny espresso macchiato instead. Not surprisingly, her espresso maker was the first thing she'd unpacked from the move. We didn't have many traditions in the Bishop household, but Friday breakfast was one of my favorites.

So far, our first full week in the new town had been both productive and uneventful. And when you move your family four states away to start new jobs and a school, uneventful is a good thing. Boxes were slowly disappearing. Shelves and closets were quickly filling up. Furniture was finally coming to rest after being tried a couple different ways. Pictures were even hung in a few of the rooms. Mostly Ben's. His room had been our initial focus. Cheryl and I felt so bad about moving him a month into the fourth grade, we wanted him to feel at home as quickly as possible. Probably too much so. We'd allowed him more say in his room's décor than had ever been the case. The dark blue walls and robot video game posters were all his idea, despite early objections from both of us. It was a far cry from the bright yellow and white walls he had in Arizona. The SpongeBob curtains and *How to Train Your Dragon* posters hadn't even made the trip.

As for the new school and jobs, they'd gone about as well, if not better than I'd imagined. Ben really liked his new teacher, Mrs. Chapelfield, and seemed quick to make new friends. Cheryl was happy to finally be working the day shift and had even called on Wednesday to ask if I minded if she went out for drinks with the girls from the ER. Something she rarely got to do working the graveyard shift at the hospital in Tucson. So of course, I hadn't minded. Ben and I ordered a pizza and spent the evening huddled on the couch, watching people get voted off the island. Ben's favorite line? "The tribe has spoken."

As for myself, I was enjoying my new employment. Unlike the large firm where I'd done my internship and went on to take a position, the architectural firm here in Broken Tree was considerably smaller. So small, that I was the only landscape architect on their payroll, which thrilled me because it meant no more jockeying and vying for the more interesting landscape contracts. Every landscape contract that came across the table was mine.

Another bonus was that most of the architects at the new firm worked primarily from home, and only came into the office a couple times a week for status meetings or meetings with clients. So basically, I was enjoying the security of working for someone else and getting a steady paycheck, but with all the perks of freelance. True, gone was the prestige that goes with the glass-walled office overlooking the city skyline, but there's something to be said about working in red Coca-Cola print boxers and a wrinkled t-shirt. Not to mention the fact that I was enjoying the hell out of the new 36" LCD high-resolution monitor the new company had provided me.

With everyone settling into the new town so nicely, I was already patting myself on the back for suggesting the move to Broken Tree.

*   *   *

By the time I entered the kitchen fifteen minutes later, the sun was making its appearance through the small window over the sink. Cheryl was drying off the pancake griddle and Ben was already elbow deep in maple syrup, double-fisting crispy strips of bacon. The scene brought to mind every episode I'd seen of *Leave It to Beaver*.

"Hey, Dad!" A thin string of syrup ran down his chin as he spoke.

"Hey, Bennie," I said, and pointed to my own chin. "Napkin." I walked up behind Cheryl and wrapped my arms around her waist. She was already dressed for work and I'd always liked the way her light blue scrubs hugged her butt. Nuzzling her neck, I breathed her in deeply. "Mmm. Love that smell." I planted two very strategic kisses on her neck. "Bacon smells pretty good, too."

"You'd better get it while its hot," she said, unlocking my hands and twisting out of my grasp. "And before you say another word, I'm talking about the food."

She knew me well. And after being together for over a decade, it wasn't a surprise. Cheryl offered me a plate and a smile, both of which I gladly accepted.

Settling in at the table, I poured a long stream of maple syrup onto my stack of pancakes and watched with a child's excitement as it mixed with the already melting butter.

"So what do you have going on this weekend, big guy? Any plans?"

Ben replied with a simple shrug, as noncommittal as any nine-year-old boy should be. "Probably just hang with my bros from school."

"Bros?" I asked, trying hard to keep from busting out. "Since when do you have 'bros'?"

"That's what all the guys call their friends around school."

"Hear that, Hun?" A forkful of syrupy pancake hovered in front of my mouth. "Our little boy has bros."

Cheryl threw us a sideways grin as she snapped the lid onto a plastic tub of butter. "That's great, Bennie."

"What else have you learned from the kids at school?" I asked. "Anything we need to be aware of?"

"Hmmm..." Ben tapped a sticky fork against his forehead in thought, leaving four tiny, yet distinct dots of syrup every time he pulled the fork away. I had to suppress a smile as he continued. "I learned that if you spit off the bridge on Devlin Street, it takes four seconds for it to hit the rocks."

Eyebrows raised, I offered a 'wow, very impressive' look while I chewed a mouthful. Boys are so easily entertained at that age. Life is so simple.

"There's also a place here where they show a movie on the side of a building and you watch it from your car. They sell popcorn and soda and candy and other stuff, too."

"Really? We'll have to check that out."

"Yeah, but they said it's already closed for the year."

I remembered the drive-in; the crackling speakers, the dangerously rickety playground up front. The cars full of necking teenagers that would have me giggling as my father led me on trips to the restroom. I also remember my own parents cuddling up in the front seat during the second, more adult oriented movie, while I pretended to be asleep in the back seat. They were highly affectionate people, both toward me, and especially each other, and it was Cheryl's belief that's where I got it. Unlike most young boys who are grossed out by seeing their parents that way, I actually liked seeing my parents carry on the way they did. For some reason, it made me feel safe, like nothing could ever come between them the way I'd seen it happen with other kids' parents, and I tried to always offer that same comfort to Ben.

"Oh," Ben continued, "and everyone says there's a ghost of a kid in some old cemetery here in town."

I felt my eyes widen as I nearly choked on a mouthful of golden sponge. Thankfully, I was able to work it out and into my napkin. Reaching for my glass of water, I shot a glance at Cheryl who was too busy wiping down the stove to pay much attention to our conversation. I sensed the rising of something long hidden trying to rear its head.

"Look, Dad. Mom put chocolate chips in *my* pancakes," Ben teased. "Guess you haven't been good like me 'cause you didn't get any."

"Wait a sec," I said, setting my now empty glass back on the table and pushing my plate away. I turned squarely toward my son and tried to keep my voice from sounding too anxious. "Let's back up. What's this about a kid or a ghost?"

Ben shrugged. "They said he's a little boy who died in the cemetery. Been living there ever since. They said he's waiting for his friends to come back and save him."

My eyes were assuredly the size of the silver dollar pancakes Cheryl was fond of making. I'd stopped breathing. "Save him from what?"

"Don't know. Being dead?"

I'd only managed a couple bites up to that point, but that small amount of spongy gold was enough to harden into a hot ball of lead in my stomach. Subconsciously, I slid a hand over my belly and rubbed back and forth. Something was taking a battering ram to a door that was doing all it could to hold it back.

"What happened to this little boy?" I asked, fairly certain I already knew the answer. What I was uncertain of was how far down this rabbit hole I wanted to take my nine-year-old son.

"I dunno," Ben said. "They just said he lives in some room or something in the cemetery." Growing bored with the conversation, Ben busied himself making swirls in a pool of syrup with his last morsel of bacon.

Room? Or did they mean receiving vault?

All I could do was stare at him in disbelief. Memories and long forgotten fears now steamrolled through my mind, running roughshod over anything that got in their way. Was it strictly a legend, like the ones told in every small town? Or did the story these children recited have some validity, some base in truth? Was it possible?

Connor?

"Was the ghost boy there when you were a kid, Dad?"

All at once, I grew cold and sweaty like I had been stricken with a fast working flu virus. My hands felt clammy and I wiped them on my pants. I had told Ben and Cheryl that I'd lived in Broken Tree when I was a kid, but had never mentioned Connor's name to either of them, nor what had happened to my friend that night in the cemetery. I had never discussed the circumstances to anyone other than a couple of therapists early on and to a lesser degree, my parents. It was one memory I'd always been more than happy to keep to myself.

Cheryl approached and clapped her hands, jolting me from

my trance.

"Come on, kiddo," she said. "Let's get you cleaned up and off to school."

Ben rose from the table and took his plate over to the sink. Cheryl clapped her hands a second time near his bottom and he bolted squealing from the room.

"Wash your hands and face!" Cheryl called after him. Then she bent down, kissed me on top of the head and followed Ben out of the room.

I barely acknowledged their exit.

Chapter Three

A dismal, windowless corner of a basement wasn't the best place for a home office, but it was the best I had for the time being. Working around a cluster of cardboard boxes, my fingers flew across the keyboard, Googling like there was a gun to my head. Like my life depended on it. With Cheryl at work and Ben at school, I had the house to myself and it was damn quiet. Too damn quiet, in fact. I reached over and flipped on my iPod dock and in seconds, the distortion of Nirvana's "The Man Who Sold the World" began its haunting oratory; one of the few instances of a cover outshining the original.

I was due to have a lunch meeting with a coworker to discuss the project he and I were partnered on, but first I had some research to do. By the light of a putrid table lamp and the computer monitor itself, I searched the names, first individually, then in combinations.

Connor Westphal…

Broken Tree…

Nothing came up at first. At least nothing more relevant than a tree planting ceremony for a fallen soldier over in Westphal County. Then, buried deep on the third page of search returns, I came across a link to an old story in the local newspaper. It was dated September 18th, 1987, and my eyes lit up like I'd just found out the numbers on my lottery ticket were a match.

Line by line, I devoured the details of a story I'd been shielded from all my life, suddenly asking myself why I'd never thought to look it up before now. Perhaps I never had a reason to. Or, maybe the part of me that's always right and likes to brag about it, knew it was best to leave well enough alone.

Though the details were twenty-five years old, I read them with an enthusiasm usually reserved for the day's top headlines. The setting of the article was Broken Tree, and specifically the cemetery. Connor was mentioned in the story both by name and descriptive identifiers:

Victim.

Deceased.

Body.

There were allusions to Nick and I, but we were never mentioned by name. The limited knowledge of criminal journalism I'd gained from television told me this was to protect our identities as minors, but that was an assumption. Only two lines in the story even referenced us:

'*The deceased was believed to be playing in the cemetery with two other minors at the time of his murder. The friends, both of whom are also twelve-years-old, apparently did not witness the crime and neither are considered suspects.*'

I remembered talking to an officer that morning, something I couldn't forget despite many years attempting to. As I perused the article further, it mentioned an Officer Cecil Wilson. Had he been the one who'd come to my parent's house that morning, breaking the news that would change our lives forever? Considering Broken Tree was such a small town and homicides were a rarity, I wondered if it changed his life as well.

Key phrases stood out from the rest of the text, catching my attention and holding it like several tiny car wrecks one right after the other:

Like nothing I've ever seen.

Simply inhumane.

An anonymous neighbor was quoted, asking what kind of person could do such a thing.

Only one other phrase in the preliminary article caught my attention: *person of interest*. It wasn't until an article I found dated several weeks later, that I learned of someone actually being arrested for what happened to Connor. *What happened.* Still couldn't bring myself to refer to it any other way. Even though "what happened" hardly described the brutality of Connor Westphal's fate. Old habits, I guess.

Jerry Lee Evans.

A vagrant with quite a lengthy rap sheet, Evans had been seen hanging around the cemetery a few nights before the discovery of Connor's body. He'd even been reported to the authorities more than once. When the police picked him up, they reported it looked as if Evans had been squatting inside the cemetery's abandoned receiving vault. The iron door was so poorly deteriorated that it was practically rusting off the hinges, thus allowing him access. According to the article, Evans was subsequently booked on a vagrancy charge, but released on his own recognizance.

Really? I thought. *Released to where?*

According to testimony, Evans was dropped off at the cemetery only hours after being picked up with stern orders from the sheriff's office to gather his things and be on his way. Obviously, he didn't heed those orders, and the good people of Broken Tree took less than an hour to come back with a guilty verdict in the murder of one of their children. With a sentence of seventy years, the fifty-two-year-old Evans was sent to a prison upstate. Less than a year later, Evans was found with a makeshift knife stuck in his gut, its mattress spring handle broken off for good measure. It was said that he died on a filthy tile floor, steaming hot water and blood pooling around him. Alone. *The same way he'd left Connor.* Reports of the words 'baby killer' written in blood on the shower wall could not be corroborated.

The loud 'PING' of the notification alert almost put me through the roof. If jumping out of my skin were at all physically possible, I would have had a flesh-colored tuxedo to hang in my closet. I turned down the volume on my computer and made a mental note to have a discussion about personal property with Ben when he got home. Taking an extra beat for my heart to calm, I checked my computer screen and saw that I had one hour until my meeting. Just enough time to get some work done.

*   *   *

My coworker had been right. Ted's Grill did burn one hell of a burger.

"So, it sounds like we're on the same page," Mark said, tossing his napkin onto his plate, covering the remnants of his lunch. The local branch of the Veterans of Foreign Wars had commissioned a fountain to be erected in the park to commemorate the fallen soldiers from Broken Tree. The number of lost since WWI was staggering, but that's how it always seemed to be with small towns. I was designing the layout of the memorial and surrounding green space while Mark was handling the marble slabs and brickwork for the paths. It wasn't exactly his job, but he'd volunteered to help the newbie until I got more settled in. I wasn't ready to take the torch and run with it only a week into the new job.

"Think so," I said, tossing my own napkin onto my plate; the universal signal for our server to come get our plates and drop off the bill.

"Great. So how's everything else going? All unpacked?"

"Getting there," I said with a nod. "Everything's going pretty smoothly." At least it was until this morning, I thought. "I do have a question for you, though. Pretty off topic."

"Shoot," he said. "Name on my driver's license says 'Open Book.'"

"Well, Mr. Book, how long have you lived in Broken Tree?"

"Oh, shit." Mark leaned back in his chair, grabbed his nearly empty glass of iced tea and swirled the ice around. "It's gotta be eleven, twelve years, I guess. Had to get out of Minneapolis. Why do you ask?"

"Ever heard stories about some ghost that's apparently haunting the cemetery?"

Our server appeared at the table. Looking well into his early thirties, the man seemed kind of old to be working the lunch shift at a greasy spoon. He reminded me of an actor who takes the day job to pay the bills until their acting career takes off. But this was small town Minnesota, not LA or New York, and I wasn't sure Hollywood made long distance calls.

"Can I get you guys anything else?" the server named Oliver asked.

Mark and I shook our heads in response as Oliver started gathering our plates off the table.

Lines creased Mark's forehead. "Which cemetery we talking?"

Good question. Obviously, there were more than one, even in such a small town.

"You're probably talking about the one out on 36," Mark continued when I failed to answer. "It's Azalea Avenue through town, turns into 36 once you get out of the city limits. At least that's the only one I've ever heard any spook stories about."

"That's probably the one," I said. *Spook stories?* My heart rate rose a notch.

"I'll be right back with your checks," Oliver said, and turned away, but not until after hesitating for a beat. He'd taken just long enough to give both Mark and I sidelong looks, like he wanted to say something.

"My kids talk about it from time to time," Mark went on. "I figure every small town has a ghost story or two. Something to keep kids from hangin' out in the cemetery. Drinking. Screwing and whatnot. Why? You hear something different?"

"Not really," I said. "Kid mentioned it this morning. Was wondering if there was anything to it."

Oliver returned and stood the thin book that housed our lunch bill up on the edge of the table.

"I got this," Mark said, swiping the little book before I could. "Anyway, never really put much stock into ghosts, boogeymen or teenage girls possessed by century-old demons. I doubt there's anything going on out there. Nothing more than urban legends."

"I think they're true."

We both looked up to find Oliver still standing next to the table. He didn't appear to be waiting, but he didn't seem in a hurry to go away, either.

"I'm sorry," I asked, unsure I'd heard him right.

"The stories. About the ghost of the kid in the cemetery." Oliver's eyes were more alert than I'd seen them up to that point. The ever-present joviality he'd served us with over the past hour was gone. "There was a kid who got killed out there. About twenty-five years or so ago. I actually grew up next door to his parents. I was a little younger than the kid, but I remember them. Nice enough. Occasionally I'd see them out in the yard or my parents would be doing something and stop to talk to them. Seemed sad underneath the smiles, though, which is completely understandable."

To say that I was caught completely off guard by Oliver's admission would be like saying snow was cold. Not only was I taken aback, but I was utterly captivated by what he had to say.

"Do you know if they're still around?" I asked. "The parents?"

Oliver shook his head. "Left town when I was in high school. I guess they dealt with their kid's death well enough, but according to my parents who talked to the Westphals before they left, it was all the stories and rumors making their way around town about their son haunting the cemetery that eventually drove them out. Can't say I blame them. Man, that had to be tough."

Westphals. So we were definitely talking about the same kid at least.

"So what about these stories?" I caught myself chewing on my thumbnail. A habit I thought I'd kicked.

Oliver cast a glance toward the kitchen area and nodded his head to someone. "I gotta move along," he said almost apologetically. "But basically, there were reports of animal carcasses being discovered all over the cemetery. Grounds crew were always finding them. They also told stories about hearing things in the cemetery, and feeling like they were being followed around. Got to the point nobody wanted to work there. People stopped setting foot on the grounds period. Eventually, they just locked the place up and shut it down to future burials. Never went out there myself, but I had friends who did. They could tell you stories."

"Wow," Mark said once Oliver had walked away with the bill and Mark's credit card. "So this has been interesting." He offered a chuckle while drumming his wallet on the table. "Unfortunately, I gotta run. Otherwise I'd love to sit here and swap ghost stories all day. But, I need to get home and let the kids' new puppy out before she pisses on my wife's Persian rug. Again."

I nodded, but didn't say anything more on the topic of ghosts or the cemetery. We simply made small talk for another minute or two until Oliver returned with Mark's credit card. The server didn't stick around to chat anymore and that was fine with me. Between the newspaper articles and what Oliver had shared not only about the ghost rumors, but about Connor's parents, I had more going around in my head than I could process.

Minutes later, while sitting in my car out in the parking lot, I found myself equally fascinated and terrified by all of it. But, it was Mark's words that echoed loudest in my mind: *Something to keep kids from hangin' out in the cemetery.* How ironic. And it had taken all of a week for the past to catch up with me.

Checking my watch, I realized I had enough time to make a stop before heading home to meet Ben at the bus stop. I only hoped I had the nerve.

Chapter Four

I wasn't the only one who'd grown up in the last twenty-five years. The town of Broken Tree was considerably more expansive now than when I was a kid, though still not big enough to be referred to as anything but a town. So much had changed from when I'd last called this place home. Things had progressed. Where there used to be a gas station that sold an occasional bottle of soda, there was now a full-fledged mini grocery that happened to sell gas. Independent hardware stores, having fallen by the wayside as the big boys moved in, were now upscale daycare centers and nail salons. It was the continual evolution and necessary recycling of the American small town. Part of the American Dream was owning one's own business, and empty storefronts provided the perfect opportunity.

But all this change made finding the cemetery difficult.

I drove through my old neighborhood for twenty minutes, getting the sense I'd passed my childhood home more than once. I'd see a house that looked familiar, then a house that looked identical would turn up on the next street over. Twenty-five years erased a lot of clarity, and I couldn't have picked out the house I'd grown up in if a gun had been put to my head. Luckily, my childhood home wasn't what I was trying to find.

About the time frustration started setting in, I turned yet another corner and noticed a large field behind some houses with a grouping of treetops off in the distance. From what I remembered, the old cemetery had almost as many trees as gravesites. This was Minnesota after all.

I turned left down the next street, took it a block and turned right when it intersected with Azalea, the street Mark had mentioned that turned into route 36. Four blocks later, the housing development stopped abruptly. It was as if the builders had run out of wood and drywall, and instead of getting more, had simply packed up and moved on. I crested the hill beyond the last house on the lane, passing a white and black Route 36 sign with the obligatory buckshot holes grouped in the center.

And that's when I saw it for the first time in twenty-five years. As much as the town had grown, it appeared the old cemetery still remained on the outskirts. Progress had expanded the city limits over the years, but apparently, only in all other directions.

The cemetery, still enclosed by an eight-foot tall iron fence, crept up on my right as I slowly approached. Letting off the gas and flipping on my turn signal, I pulled onto the short turn around alongside the fence and came to a stop. The black iron gate still watched over the entrance, just as it had so many years ago, its spires ending in points like a line of upright arrows. The high schoolers in Broken Tree liked to say the monolithic gate was there to ensure that what was inside stayed inside. The younger kids like myself pretended not to believe them, but deep down, we weren't sure. Towering oak trees, their leaves starting to turn, still guarded the cemetery's perimeter like sentries stationed strategically. In fact, except for looking more crowded, everything about the cemetery still looked as I remembered.

In some aspects, it was like I never left. All I had to do was close my eyes and I could easily put myself back there. Back to that night. Back before "what happened"…

*   *   *

Connor pushed his glasses further up the bridge of his nose. I could tell he was weighing the benefits against the consequences. It was classic Connor. Always thinking too much.

"I don't know guys," he said. "It's later than usual."

Nick wasn't only the opposite of the always-cautious Connor, but he was generally the instigator of our trio. Not to mention a semi-professional button pusher who prided himself on being able to get a rise out of Connor and me. Nick rarely took no for an answer, and tonight was no different.

"Come on, Conner." Nick threw up his hands. "We've played hide and seek in the cemetery tons of times. And most were at night."

Connor hitched his pants and scanned the downtown streets, first in one direction then the other. A signature stall tactic. Finally, he turned to me.

"What do you think, Adam?" Connor asked, his eyes unsure. "Isn't it awfully late?"

I stood on the sidewalk drinking the bottle of Yoo-Hoo I'd swiped from Johnson's Stop & Go. I wasn't exactly a thief, I simply took liberties from time to time like most kids will when unsupervised. I knew it was wrong. But I'd also heard my mother complain more than once that, with the prices he was charging, Old Man Johnson was robbing us blind anyway. So I just looked at taking the Yoo-Hoo as making us a little more square.

Like I said: liberties.

As for going to the cemetery, I was game, so I sided with Nick and shrugged off Connor's concern.

"Isn't it *usually* late when we hang in the cemetery?" I asked.

Reluctantly, Connor nodded. "But—"

"And, at this point," I interrupted, glancing up at the digital 11:10 displayed on the bank sign across the street, "won't you already have to sneak back into your house?"

Again, Connor had no choice but to agree.

"Okay then," I said, tossing the empty bottle into a nearby trashcan. "What's it matter how late it is?"

Connor took a minute to consider his response, looking from me to Nick, then back to me again. I wasn't sure if it was because his father had lost two fingers in an accident at work, or if it was just his nature, but Connor was by far the most cautious of the three of us. Probably the most cautious kid in our school. This very scene had played out in one form or another a million times before, each of us playing these exact same roles.

"Alright then," Connor muttered, having no doubt run through all of the possible worst-case scenarios in his mind and coming to the conclusion that disappointing his buddies was at the top of that list. "But, I'm not *It*."

"Not *It*!" Nick blurted out a half second before I did, which wasn't unusual. It actually happened more often than not. He laughed and punched me in the arm, which also happened more often than not. So at the cemetery, our new roles will have been cast: Nick and Connor were supposed to hide.

And I was supposed to find them.

"Ninety-eight…ninety-nine…one hundred!" I shouted to a darkened cemetery a half hour later. "Ready or not, assholes, here I come!"

The cemetery grew still as the echo of my shout died away. The only remaining sound was the occasional chirping of a cricket in the early autumn night. Not even the breeze blew hard enough to rustle the leaves that were showing signs of turning. All was calm.

After having my eyes closed for so long, it took a few seconds for them to adjust to the intricate darkness of a moonlit night in which the moonlight casts deeper shadows from the leaning headstones; large ornately carved mausoleums take on the look of miniature medieval castles; trees so plentiful that one silhouette blends into another. For a cemetery that already looked creepy during the day, it donned a downright sinister veil at night. An implied danger awaited anyone brave enough to seek it out.

Which, of course, was the draw for young boys on the verge of teen-dom.

I set out in search of my friends, their favorite hiding places front and center in my mind. It never failed; when you share your secrets with fellow hiders, it came back to bite you in the butt the next time those hiders became the seeker. This was a lesson the three of us were slow to learn. That's how I knew Nick was hiding either behind one of the large trees or one of the various clumps of bushes scattered throughout the cemetery; both ideal places.

As for Connor, it was well known that his favorite place to hide was under one of the small footbridges that crossed over a shallow creek. As smart and prudent as Connor was, imaginative he was not. In the eight or nine times we had played the game in the cemetery, Connor had hidden under the bridge at least half of them, thinking that we wouldn't expect him to hide there again. But he was wrong. At this point, we knew more often than not that he *would* hide there again. Again and again, in fact. The other footbridge that crossed the stream on the other side of the cemetery, was located entirely too close to the receiving vault for any of us, much less Connor, to utilize as a hiding place. It was simply too creepy to go near. Typically, any hole dug into the side of a hill, with its overrun ivy and crumbling walls of stone, was a place kids would want to explore. But when you consider what it had been used for back in the day—storing dead bodies during the winter when the ground was too hard to dig—you couldn't have come up with a better child repellent.

So with all of this in mind, Connor's bridge was the first place I headed. Making my way along the edge of the cemetery, I was mindful to sidestep the areas where a few leaves had already started falling. Nothing gives you away in a game of outdoor hide and seek faster than crunching leaves. As I crept along the fence line toward Connor, I scanned the cemetery grounds, keeping a vigilant eye out for Nick and a trained ear out for Connor, who had a habit of giggling to himself as he hid. He couldn't help it. That's the kind of kid he was.

As I neared the footbridge, I slowed my pace and eased up onto the edge. The wood planks, worn with age, made the faintest of creaking sounds as I stepped onto the first one. Thankfully, it wasn't enough to give away my position. The groan could have easily been made by a gust of wind. After momentarily listening for any telltale signs my cover had been blown, I slowly tiptoed up the ramp to the top of the arch. Thanks to an especially dry summer, the shallow creek bed below was bone dry, nothing in it but crinkled leaves. My plan was to jump down into the creek bed and scare the living shit out of my friend. I had to stifle my own giggle as I watched the scene play out in my mind.

With my toes perched on the edge, I took the stance of an Olympic diver, though there were no back flips in my future. Glancing down, I judged the distance at around five feet or so. A manageable height. With a deep breath and my heart pounding, I pushed off. It took a whole second for my feet to hit the soft ground. Bending at the knees, and with my arms outstretched, I yelled, "Gotcha!" But the only thing I found under that bridge was the hollow echo of my voice fading in the emptiness.

*   *   *

A horn shrieked.

A gust rocked my car.

My eyes opened to an old blue pickup swerving around my back end, which judging by the prolonged horn blast, was apparently jutting out onto the road. With my heart racing, and white-knuckled hands on the steering wheel, I watched the truck diminish in size as it rolled on down the road. A half-mile away, it took a curve and disappeared beyond a strip of trees that marked the edge of a sugar beet field.

With the memory reluctantly fading from my mind and a thin film of sweat coating my face, I closed my eyes and took a deep breath. It was a good five minutes before I could safely rule out a heart attack. Even then, I wasn't sure a year or two hadn't been erased from my life.

My eyes once again open, I checked the road in both directions. Slowly pulling onto the pavement, I made a U-turn away from the cemetery. For a quarter mile, the towering gate of iron loomed in my rearview mirror like something nightmares are made of. Then, like a ship sinking to the depths of the ocean, it begrudgingly faded into my past, though I had a feeling it wasn't once and for all.

Chapter Five

He pushed imaginary glasses further up onto his nose, an old habit, and watched the black sedan pull away with a renewed excitement. A child's excitement. Even though the man never got out of his car, the presence of his old friend was something Connor Westphal could simply feel. The way his spirit was felt by every tree, shrub and blade of grass in this necropolis he was forced to called home. It was similar to a twin sensing something was wrong with their sibling, despite the fact many miles might separate them. It's felt in their gut. Adam Bishop may not be twelve-years-old anymore, not like himself, but who could be better company than an old friend? For so long he had waited for his friends to return for him. For so long he had ached, desperate for their companionship. He had the power to make it happen. He had learned over time that he could take creatures out of their own world and bring them into his. Squirrels, rabbits and that one coyote. But, he had always been hesitant to do to another human being what had been done to him. But, the longer he remained alone in his world, the more his anger and resentment grew. The more the living taunted him. Twenty-five years was long enough. He was ready.

Welcome back, my friend. Good to see you.

Chapter Six

"You know, this works better when both parties take an active role." Cheryl emerged from beneath the burgundy and beige-striped comforter and propped herself up against the headboard. Without hesitation, she pulled the sheet up, covering her bare chest. Cheryl's modesty, even after a decade of marriage, was just one of the many things I found endearing about the woman. The list, quite frankly, would fill up an entire notebook. "Am I doing something wrong?" she asked. "Usually, you're more into this."

"Sorry," I said, simply because she was right. Usually, I was more into it. Way more. Like a kid with cavities is into candy. Tonight, however, she'd spent a full twenty minutes under the covers with no real response or feedback on my part. In fact, all she had gotten for her efforts, was a thin sheen of sweat and an incredible need for a drink of water.

My mind was definitely elsewhere. I couldn't concentrate. Not that I really needed to in my position, but it helped if my mind was at least in the same room. Tonight it wasn't. Tonight it was in a cold, dark cemetery on the edge of town. Hell, it may as well have been on another planet.

"It's not you, babe." I reached up and brushed away some of her damp hair so that I could see her eyes. "It's me. Totally me."

She reached across me and scooped up the glass of water that was sitting on my nightstand. The sheet fell away and a flicker of excitement coursed through my loins when her bare breasts pressed against my stomach. At least I knew I wasn't dead.

"Oh." She offered a wry smile. "Are we playing 'name that cliché' tonight?"

I reached for the remote on the nightstand and turned down the television that had been nothing more than a mask for those "grown up" sounds you don't want your nine-year-old to hear.

"I need to talk," I said, but not until releasing a long, drawn out sigh. *Here goes.*

Her eyebrows arched as she emptied the glass of water and handed it back to me. "Wait," she said, eyebrows cocked over wide eyes. "*You* need to talk, or *we* need to talk?"

Recognizing her alarm, I shook my head and put my hand on her covered thigh.

"I do," I said. "But feel free to interject from time to time." My attempt at a chuckle was incredibly weak. Even after a deep, stalling breath, I still didn't know where to begin; didn't know how much to tell her. So eventually I made it easy on myself. I started from the beginning. I told her everything about Connor, Nick and what happened that night in the cemetery. I told her about my parents moving us away and the string of subsequent therapists. I even brought her up to speed on all the information my research had uncovered earlier that day. No point in keeping it from her at this juncture. Like peeling off a Band-aid, I laid it all out there, once and for all, and braced myself for what was to come.

Not surprisingly, what was to come took a few minutes.

"My God." The pillow Cheryl clutched to her chest looked like it was being strangled. "Why on Earth would you want to come back here, Adam? If I had known, if I'd had any idea—"

"I didn't even know, babe." It was a feeble thing to interrupt with, so I felt the need to explain further. "Not really, I mean. I didn't find out what *really* happened, the full extent of it at least, until today."

"Adam…" But, it was all too overwhelming and it took her a few moments before she was of a mind to continue.

I laid beside her for quite awhile, caressing her arm and answering the multitude of questions she felt needed asked. At least I tried to. Not all of life's questions have answers, and the same was true of Cheryl's. I didn't know why we thought playing in the cemetery at night was a good idea. I didn't know why I hadn't told her about any of it sooner. And, I sure as hell didn't know why I thought this wouldn't all come up when we moved to Broken Tree.

When discussions of leaving Arizona for the Midwest first started taking place, we made a list of attributes we were looking for in a new area; a list of things that would be beneficial to raising a family. Good schools. Quiet tree-lined neighborhoods. A real sense of community. Every step of the way, with every attribute added to the list, one place kept coming to mind: Broken Tree. Despite blocking out a large chunk of my childhood at a cost of $150 an hour, I still had some fond memories of the town, hidden in those places even the therapists couldn't reach. And when judging Broken Tree against the list, I found I could put a check next to practically every box on that list. Regardless of what had happened in the past, Broken Tree had everything we were looking for and seemed like the idyllic fit for my family. Quite honestly, I saw no reason not to move here. And when, on the off chance, I looked into the want ads and saw that one of the few architectural firms in town was looking for a landscape architect, I'd taken it as a sign and returned to my childhood home. I thought the story would end there. Unfortunately, I'd been wrong.

It was sometime after one o'clock in the morning when Cheryl's well of questions finally dried up, leaving my unburdened soul laid bare. My insides felt raw. The conversation had taken a lot out of me, picking apart not only my past, but every decision I'd made since. It had apparently taken a lot out of Cheryl as well, because she'd been the first to drift off to sleep.

It was sometime afterward that my mind finally collapsed from exhaustion and I followed suit, allowing the dream to snake its way into what little room for thought remained...

*   *   *

Come on, dammit!

My twelve-year-old hands shook the window ledge with urgency. The house was old, and when the air was thick with humidity, the wooden window casing would swell so bad, you'd think it had been glued. I inched the window up a little at a time, using my palms as hammers to boost it along the way. All the while, I listened for any sounds coming from either behind me or inside the darkened house. Finally, after a couple of anxious minutes, I'd pried it open enough to squeeze myself through.

I was in my bedroom, perceivably safe and sound.

Once the window was closed and locked behind me, I stripped off my clothes and crawled under my sheets. My heart was pounding so hard, I had to plead with it to stop, fearing it was about to burst through my chest. In the morning, my mother would find me dead in a pool of blood only a horror movie could do justice to. Then I pulled the thin sheet over my head so I wouldn't have to watch the shadow of the magnolia swaying in the breeze outside my window.

"Adam…"

I let out a quick shriek and turned to find Connor Westphal, bloodied and distorted and curled up beside me. The sight of him caused another cry to escape my lips before I could stifle it. Connor's face was barely recognizable and streaked with blood and dirt, though somehow I knew it was him. Two clean trails ran from Connor's eyes where tears had washed away the muck. Those eyes that had once been blue were black as night. Dark paint-thick circles, like those you get when you haven't slept for days, surrounded his eyes. But it looked as if Connor hadn't slept in years. The left side of his face sagged like it had lost a fight with a large rock, a hole gaped where his nose had once been, and a dark red fingerling of blood ran from one ear down the length of his neck.

"Adam."

I inched away. "Holy shit, Connor! What happened?"

"Why'd you leave me there, Adam? Why'd you leave me in the cemetery?"

The way Connor's jaw hung awkwardly from his face made me wonder how he was even speaking. It shouldn't have been possible. The left side had been completely separated from the rest of his skull, creating an unnaturally cockeyed motion as it formed each word.

I shook my head.

"No," I said, anxious to finally set the story straight, despite my fear. "We waited, Connor. We called to you, I swear. We called a bunch of times. But you didn't answer. We didn't know where you were."

The child-like form eased itself ever closer to my body. "You shouldn't have left. Shame on you, Adam. Shame on you and Nick."

A piercing cold ran through my spine, but it wasn't cold like ice. It was the chill of overwhelming terror.

"But, Nick and I—"

"Look what happened to me, Adam. Look what *you* let happen."

I closed my eyes and started to plead. Despite Connor's insistence, I couldn't look. I couldn't stand to look at this, this *thing* beside me another second longer. This hideous affront had long since become anything but Connor Westphal.

"Look at me!" The heat of its breath hit me square in the face, raw and stagnant like rotting garbage from a dumpster. I gagged from the stench and opened my eyes to find the unspeakable horror pressed within an inch of my face. If there had still been a nose attached to the broken face, it would have been pressed firmly against mine.

Hands were suddenly on my face and I screamed. Fingers nipped at my eyes, prying them open.

"Look at me, Adam! Look what you let happen!"

As I desperately tried pulling away from the hands, screams poured from my mouth. How long it would take for my mother or father to come running, awoken by their son's screams as he fought for his life? My chest heaved. My throat burned. They had to hear! I was screaming so loud!

"You're gonna pay for this, Adam!" The voice coming from where the mouth used to be was no longer the kind voice of my friend. No longer a boy's voice. No longer innocent. What came at me now was pure hatred and full of spite. It was the voice itself that frightened me most, despite having seen the gaping maw from where it spewed forth.

"You're gonna suffer just like I did!"

The hands returned to my face and it made me cringe, eyes

still clamped shut. A finger snaked its way into my mouth, but I jerked away. I tried to pull the sheet off my head, but the cloth turned to dirt in my hands and collapsed down over me. Putrid soil and what I thought was compost started raining down, burying me beneath its weight.

"You're gonna suffer just like I did, Adam!"

"No!" The musty dirt filled my mouth as I cried out. "No!"

As hands tore at my face, the dirt continued to mound around me, constricting my movement. I felt my skin being ripped from my cheek, my flesh being torn. More hands clutched my arm, shaking me violently. I cried out again, pulling my arm free of its grip, spitting earth from my mouth. As I raised from my shallow grave, my eyes opened wide.

Both the dirt and the thing that used to be Connor were gone.

Cheryl's voice was soft and assuring as she tried to talk me down. "It's okay, baby. It was a dream. Just a bad, bad dream." With one hand on my chest, Cheryl stroked my cheek with the other.

Still gasping for air, I laid back. The dream had seemed so real, like it was happening right then and there. I listened to Cheryl's soothing voice, not entirely convinced that it hadn't. Taking a succession of deep breaths, I exhaled each one slowly, the taste of dirt still in my mouth, the stench of rancid breath still in my nostrils. All the while, Connor's words echoed in my mind...

You're gonna suffer just like I did.

Chapter Seven

After eventually falling back asleep, I awoke the next morning with one thought in mind: I had to track down an old friend. If I was going to deal with this situation—*guilt?*—with Connor, I needed to talk to someone other than Cheryl or a shrink. Someone who was there and who knew what I knew.

I needed to talk to Nick.

Most of my morning was consumed with work in the form of a less than encouraging teleconference, which led to me making drastic changes to the green space where the Veterans' fountain was going in. But the afternoon was spent sitting on my living room floor, laptop balanced on my knees, watching my nine-year-old rid Los Angeles of alien invaders. *Yes, I'm proud of you, son. Yes, you really blew him up good.*

When I wasn't encouraging Lieutenant Bishop in the good fight, I was searching for the whereabouts of one Nick Gant. Much to my surprise, Nick proved less elusive than a twenty-five year old news story that a small town clearly wanted to put behind them. To find Nick, all I had to do was run a search on him in The Republic's police blotter. It seems Nicholas Wilson Gant hadn't simply remained in Broken Tree, he'd kept the local police fairly busy over the years. A real one-man revenue source. It was as if Nick had taken it upon himself to keep budgetary cuts from infiltrating the Broken Tree police department.

"I made Captain!"

"Great job, Bennie! Keep it up! You'll make Colonel in no time."

I scanned the unimpressive list of offenses Nick had rung up over the years. Apparently, he was a big fan of drunk and disorderly. The implications of this, or at least what it might say about Nick's life in the aftermath of "what happened," dredged up a bit of sadness.

"Sweet!"

Like the Furies of Greek mythology, Ben's thumbs punished the buttons on the game controller. The click-clack tore my attention away from the laptop. Looking at the boy sitting on the floor beside me, I had to stifle a laugh. The look of concentration on Ben's face was as intense as I'd ever seen on a child. If he wasn't careful, Ben would spend the rest of his life without the front half of his tongue the way he clenched it between his teeth.

There are times as a parent when the sheer sight of your child can almost bring you to tears. You love them so much it hurts. That's how it was as I sat there watching Ben. It wasn't until after he'd come along that Cheryl and I found out how much room there was in the human heart for love. Still basking in that light, we decided not to wait to have another child. We went to work right away, though, to be honest, it wasn't exactly work. Six months after Benjamin Alan Bishop was born, we found out Cheryl was pregnant again. She'd broken the news to me over beef medallions and cabernet at our favorite restaurant in Tucson. It was an expensive place, and a luxury we didn't indulge in often, but special news calls for some measure of splurging.

We were so excited to be expecting again, we started doing all the fun stuff that expectant parents get to do: turning our tiny home office into a second nursery, making the big money purchases as well as the little ones like socks and a baby blanket. We got so caught up in the excitement of having another baby, that when the spotting started around month four, we completely ignored it and continued down our path. By the time we found out that Cheryl was no longer pregnant, the second nursery was already finished.

Nothing makes a miscarriage more difficult than having to look at the nursery every time you walk down the hall. The moon and stars lit up the walls by night, the sun and fluffy white clouds in the light of day. After about a month of having our hearts break every time we walked past the room, one day I just closed the door and left it closed. Cheryl didn't question it, and eventually, dealing got easier and we moved on. Life has a way of moving forward on you whether you want it to or not, especially when there's a one-year-old involved. If it's possible for some good to come from a miscarriage, Ben was the happy recipient of it. We focused all of our attention and love on our little boy like he was the only thing we had left.

Over time, Cheryl and I would eventually broach the subject of having another child. The conversation usually came up while sitting on the couch watching television. I would notice the tears running down her face whenever a diaper commercial would come on, or I'd land on one of those baby shows on TLC while channel surfing. The conversations always ended with Cheryl saying, "maybe someday." But, at some point you come to realize that "someday" isn't coming and you simply stop talking about it altogether.

And you move on.

I took the address where I would most likely find Nick and typed it into my cell phone. After kissing Ben on top of his head and wishing him continued success, I closed my laptop and got to my feet.

"I'm stepping out for a few, okay kiddo?"

"Where you goin'?" His eyes never left the television screen. His tongue retreated into his mouth only long enough to speak, then reappeared immediately after.

"To see an old friend." Strangely, I'd had to think for a moment, unsure how to refer to Nick. Ultimately, the term 'old friend' seemed as appropriate an answer as any. After all, it wasn't a lie. "Mom's in the shower and will be out soon. Don't answer the door or the phone, okay?"

"'Kay."

"Love ya, buddy."

"Love you, too, Dad."

When I left the room, Ben was still kicking ass and taking names.

Chapter Eight

With a name like Cue Balls, I wasn't sure what to expect. It could easily be a nice, upscale pool hall and bar where Broken Tree's hipster community could get their billiards on. Or it could be your typical small town joint with a follicly-challenged owner and equally balding clientele, their asses planted on the same barstools night after night like they'd taken out a lease on them. I wasn't surprised to find that Cue Balls fell into the latter category. Tight and windowless, the single room was dark, drab and pretty much the way Cheryl likes the family room when we curl up on the couch to watch a movie. Where two windows looked to have once been, pieces of painted black plywood had been put up to cover the holes. It was as if the bar's owner didn't want the outside world intruding on his customer's brief respite from their crappy lives. He probably feared the passing of the sun would remind them how much time they'd been wasting away, which might be bad for business.

I climbed onto a stool at the bar, and with my back to the counter, took closer inventory of the rest of the room. A hodge-podge of sports memorabilia and neon beer signs provided the only décor. Three beat up pool tables took up the entire left half of the room. Square tables, that no doubt wobbled when leaned on, filled in the other side with surrounding mismatched chairs. The few patrons scattered about were equally mismatched and uninteresting. I could have been in any number of dive bars littering the streets and strip malls of small town America. It was the world of dollar drafts on Tuesdays, and paychecks being cashed on Fridays to cover the week's tab.

It wasn't a world I cared to spend much time in.

Turning on my stool, I noticed a young barmaid in a black t-shirt and jeans stocking one of the coolers with bottles of cheap light beer.

"Be with you in one sec, Hon." The twenty-something barmaid flashed the flirty smile used by those in the industry all around the world. The one that said, "I'll be your best friend if you promise to remember me when it's time to pay your tab."

Returning her smile, I turned my attention to the flat screen television mounted behind the bar. An episode of Sports Center was on, and one of the suits with slick backed hair was explaining how the pennant races in baseball would benefit from the addition of another wild card spot in each league.

"So what can I get ya?" The barmaid dried her hands on a white towel tucked into the front of her jeans. Although there was no doubt it helped line her pockets with more tips, her smile also brightened what was an unnaturally dreary room, and I silently applauded her for it.

As I considered my choices, I found myself in the mood for a tall, heady pint of Guinness, a newly acquired love of mine. However, I felt it best not to stand out from this crowd. Even if this dive bar did have Guinness on tap, its patrons hardly looked the Guinness type, and ordering one would definitely mark me as a stranger to these parts. Not that anyone would recognize me. Not after all these years. But, drawing unwanted attention still seemed like the wrong play. It was better to blend in.

"Something light."

The barmaid bent over the freshly-stocked cooler and pulled out the same type of bottle she'd just put in. Twisting off the cap, she set the beer on a napkin in front of me, and any concern that the beer might not be cold dissipated. A fine mist rose up from the bottle's opening and the outside was instantly blanketed in a thin layer of frosty condensation.

"Start ya a tab?"

"Sure," I said, and got another one of her big smiles in return. She left me to my beer and the talking heads on the television. Apparently, the Anaheim Angels had clinched the division the night before, which meant my beloved Arizona Diamondbacks had missed the playoffs once again. It was the second bit of knowledge in a matter of minutes that hadn't surprised me. Not wanting to stick around too long, I took a drawn out pull from my bottle of tasteless beer and decided to get right to it.

"Excuse me," I said. "Do you know a Nick Gant?"

This time the smile seemed genuine. "Know him? Hell, I babysit him several times a week."

"You babysit for him?"

"No," she said. "I literally babysit *him*." With raised eyebrows, she nodded down the length of the bar where a disheveled man sat alone at the end, head hung down, both hands on the empty glass in front of him. I wasn't sure how I missed him when I scanned the room earlier, but like a white car stuck in a snowdrift, he was easily missed. He blended right into the bland interior of the room, which is what a lot of people actually look for in a place Cue Balls.

"Not sure who watches his kids," the barmaid continued. "They're with their mom in Florida last I heard. Tell me he didn't skip bail again. Or wait, you're not from the child support agency, are you?"

I shook my head.

"Ex-wife's attorney?"

"Absolutely not." The line of questioning would have been comical had their implications not been so sad. The more possibilities she ran through, the more depressing Nick's life sounded. "Nothing like that. I guess you could say I'm, uh, friend of a friend."

With a nod of understanding, the barmaid, whose name I still didn't know and hadn't thought to ask, went back to stocking her coolers, prepping for the evening crowd. I found myself staring at Nick, contemplating what I was going to say. What does one say to an old friend whom they hadn't seen since childhood, especially after leaving under such negative circumstances? And without a single word since. It dawned on me then that I hadn't really expected Nick to actually be here, even though, according to the police blotter, the odds were pretty good he would be. Or maybe I had *hoped* he wouldn't be, deep down where things you don't like to admit live. After stalling a few more minutes, I decided that if I didn't get on with it, I would either sit there all day, or I'd eventually talk myself out of approaching him altogether.

Picking up my beer, I slid off the stool and got on with it.

Across the room, two young men started complaining loudly about their darts not sticking in the dartboard. One said something about the board being a piece of shit and jammed a fistful of darts directly into it. Two of the darts fell back out and onto the floor. Slinging a round of curses at whomever might be in a management position, the men picked up their bottles of beer, drained them and walked out, but not before slamming the bottles down onto a nearby table.

I waited until the round of subsequent murmurs died down

before making my way to the end of the bar. Nick appeared not to have even noticed the ruckus. Either he had already drunk enough to dull his senses, or that kind of outburst was common in this place and didn't warrant his attention. My guess, it was probably a combination of the two.

"This seat taken?" I asked, but got no response. "Excuse me." When that didn't garner any reaction either, I looked up at the barmaid who made no attempt to hide the fact she was watching. She shrugged. I shrugged. Then I helped myself to the stool beside this stranger whom I had once known as well as one might know a brother.

Perched on the stool like he wouldn't be comfortable anywhere else, Nick looked nothing like what I'd imagined based on my memories of the boy with whom I'd spent the first twelve years of my life. His drab, brown hair hung in clumps over his ears and looked like it hadn't seen shampoo in days. Premature grey ran rampant. His dark blue pants and matching shirt suggested a uniform of some sort, perhaps a mechanic's or factory worker. His sleeves revealed smudges of black grease.

Nick had been raised by his grandparents since the age of six. His father had drunk himself to death in between stints in the unemployment line, and his mother had run off six months later with one of the men who had literally helped dig her husband's grave. Even at the age of twenty-nine, she'd been ill prepared to be a single mother. At least that's how my mother had explained it to me. Nick's grandparents, however, were pleasant enough people, and no doubt did the best they could under the circumstances. It wouldn't be surprising, though, if they had struggled to deal with Nick had he not dealt well with what happened to Connor. And given their advanced ages, it was quite possible they'd even left him before he was truly equipped to be on his own.

"Excuse me." Enough time had passed that I figured it worthwhile to try again. But still I got nothing. With his hair falling over his face, I wondered if Nick was even awake. I ordered another beer and decided to wait. Asleep or not, he had to show signs of life at some point. Even if that meant waiting around until they kicked him out at closing time. How'd the song go? "You don't have to go home, but you can't stay here."

A moment later, a sharp crash shattered the somberness that had ahold of the room. I jumped at the sudden intrusion and nearly fell off my stool. Behind the bar, the bartender stood over a broadcast display of broken glass. The clear shards told me it had once been a pint glass. Her wry smile told me it hadn't necessarily been an accident, and I returned the smile.

Nick rubbed his face with fingers whose nails were outlined with black. When he started making guttural sounds in his throat, I felt myself cringe. I had no idea what he was doing, but it didn't sound natural.

"Hey, Molly," he mumbled through a mouthful of gravel. "Bum a cigarette?"

"Now you know you can't smoke in here. You ain't been asleep that long, Van Winkle." The barmaid, whose name I now knew was Molly, chided Nick, but offered me the smile. "The law hasn't changed in the last half hour."

His mumbled response sounded very much like "fuck." He then followed up with something even less intelligible, though with no less enthusiasm.

I cleared my throat with as much exaggeration as possible. "Bullshit law, huh? Next thing you know you won't even be allowed to smoke in your own home." My argument was feigned. Pure unadulterated bullshit. In all honesty, I abhorred the smell of cigarette smoke. Always had. I was actually glad when states started passing smoking bans in bars and restaurants. But Nick didn't know that.

He looked up at me, studied my face with red and puffy eyes. I wasn't sure if he was trying to place me, or his eyes were simply having trouble focusing. After an awkward moment, he looked away without uttering a word. But I'd had his attention long enough to get a good look at his face as well, and my God, he looked at least twenty years older than me, despite our identical ages. What startled me the most were the sunken lines creasing his face like the veins on a leaf, crisscrossing back and forth, going this way and that. His face reminded me of an old sailor whose weathered features had born one too many storms.

With all the hours I'd spent on a therapist's couch, how many of them had I spent wondering about Nick and how well he and his grandparents had dealt with "what happened?" I didn't even know whether they had stayed in Broken Tree or not. But, I could see now that they had most definitely stayed, and Nick's life had taken the proverbial brunt of it.

I watched SportsCenter for a few more minutes trying to find the right way to strike up a conversation about a cemetery and the ghost of a kid we both knew. I'd spent the entire day shuffling through ideas, but none of them seemed any more plausible than another. When the topic of the smoking ban fell into my lap, I had thought for sure I'd gotten a foot in the door. But, that match had burnt out without igniting a single word from the man next to me.

I considered other topics, like asking him if he was a Twins or a Vikings fan, but that didn't seem like a path that would lead the conversation where I needed it to go. Talking sports would be a fruitless endeavor, as would most topics, I began to realize. How do you bring up a conversation about a dead boy's ghost with someone who had not only known that boy on a personal level, but had been present when the crossover to ghost had taken place.

I finally decided that, sometimes, the best approach is the straightforward kind.

"So, Molly, is it?" I asked, when she brought another beer for me and a shot of whiskey for Nick. "My kid was telling me there's supposedly a ghost living in the old cemetery out on 36. You believe that?"

I had started the conversation with Molly, but one sideways glance at Nick told me it was going to end with him having the last word. The knuckles on his hand turned white as the grip on his shot glass tightened. He sat up straighter, visibly focused, and once again looked my way. And that's when I knew I had him. The bait had been set, he'd swallowed it whole, and I was about to reel him in.

"Yeah, I've heard the stories," Molly said, sweeping up the last of the broken glass. "Not sure I believe it. Never experienced it for myself. But then I'm not dumb enough to go out there."

"Oh, it's true, alright," chimed Nick, suddenly very much alert. One look in his wide eyes, and it was obvious this was a topic he could get up close and personal with.

"Really?" I asked, drumming up a fair amount of skepticism. "You think so?" I could feel my heart rate slowly elevating, my hands growing clammy. I couldn't believe I was sitting in a bar in Broken Tree having this conversation out in the open. And with Nicholas Gant of all people.

Nick also seemed a little struck by it because his already pale face was beginning to take on a grey, ashen tone. I looked up at Molly, and put on an amused look. It was a façade, pure and simple. Nothing about the upcoming conversation would amuse me. But knowing no better, Molly smiled and threw me a "here we go again" wink.

"He's there," Nick said, his voice now barely above a whisper. "I go out there sometimes. To the cemetery. And I stand outside the fence. I won't go passed the gate, but I can hear him. I can hear Connor calling out to me. Calling my damn name."

Connor.

The moment I heard the name slurred from Nick's lips, something not so fleet of foot danced down my spine. The reality that was old news to Nick was becoming more real to me with every sentence of the conversation. My sweaty hands now trembled, and I put them in my lap so neither Molly nor Nick would notice.

"Connor?" I returned Molly's wink, even as I felt my insides start to cramp. It was like I was back in high school, sitting down to an exam that I hadn't studied for. The knot in my stomach grew increasingly tighter and someone other than myself had control of the rope.

"The ghost," Nick said. "His name's Connor."

"And how do you know this?" I felt like I was about to be kicked in the chest, and braced for impact. The game I was playing frightened me; moreso than not knowing.

Nick turned and looked me straight in the eye, as if measuring my intentions. I was sure his word had been called into question many times before. Not this time, though, old buddy. Not by me. In fact, I might be the only person in this entire town, that believed him.

Believed every fucking word.

"I was there," Nick said, his voice still low and gravelly. His eyes searched mine with something resembling either recognition or relief, and I pulled away slightly. I may have looked familiar to him. Or, I looked like a rare believer in the tale he had to tell. Either way, something in my eyes must have encouraged him.

"I was there the night he died!" Nick's sudden outburst sent me further back on my stool. "That's why he calls to me! All those years ago, I was there!"

Apparently, Molly couldn't hold in her laughter any longer, because she let it out freely. "You're too much, Nick Gant," she said. "I'd cut you off, but I know you well enough to know it wouldn't matter." Molly slapped the bar with her hand and turned away, walking down to the other end. She'd officially had enough of this conversation.

And frankly, so had I. All the questions I'd thought about asking had suddenly vanished. I had my answers, at least enough corroboration to satisfy my curiosity. Not to mention further my desire to investigate. It was true. If there was really a ghost in the old cemetery, it was definitely Connor.

And after all these years, he was still waiting for his friends.

Town drunk or not, I knew enough of the backstory to realize that, not only did this hollowed out shell of a man believe what he was saying, but Nick was telling the truth. Regardless who else, if anyone, believed him. And that was the funny thing about truth: belief in it was neither a contributing factor nor a requirement.

I slid off my stool, willing my legs to hold me up. They trembled so much that I wasn't sure they'd get me to the door. But my sudden desire to leave was more of a need at this point. Reaching into my wallet, I pulled out two twenties. One to cover my beer, the other to help with Nick's tab, whatever it might add up to. I was sure it would help. Besides, it was the least I could do for interrupting his solace by plunging him back into his painful past. *Our* past. Because like it or not, it was indeed something we shared. If the only thing.

I patted Nick Gant on the shoulder, torn between offering him a ride home and leaving him where he undoubtedly felt most comfortable. This is where he chose to deal with his fear and guilt. This was his shelter, a barstool and a bottle of whiskey. Molly and Cue Balls' cast of regulars were the closest thing Nick had to friends, and they humored him and his story simply because they had nowhere better to be and the entertainment was cheap.

But my circumstances were more fortunate than Nick's, and even with the seed of guilt starting to sprout, I knew I didn't want to get involved with this man. I couldn't. Not now. I had Cheryl, Ben, and my own sanity to think about. Still, my guilty conscience tugged at my resolve and I needed to escape the feeling. So I lifted my hand off his shoulder, walked out of Cue Balls and never looked back. I was afraid the ghost of our old friendship would be following me to the door, reaching out from beyond the grave.

Chapter Nine

It was near dusk in mid-October and in the rearview mirror, exhaust steam drifted up from the car's tail pipe. As the sun started to set, the evening air turned downright crisp. Minnesota would be getting its first snow before long, and I made a mental note to pick up the essentials.

Despite the car's heater set on high, I still felt a chill. I rubbed my hands together in front of the vent. The rush of warmth caused the skin on my hands to prickle, but helped little else. Taking in a monstrously deep breath, I let it out slowly and turned off the car's ignition. I knew what needed to be done, but I wasn't looking forward to it. I felt like a death row inmate with my legs being shackled in preparation for the long walk. Only I wasn't in need of a priest to walk beside me, mumbling his way through a prayer he only used for one specific occasion.

My meeting with Nick hadn't quite gone as planned. But then, I hadn't much of a plan to begin with. All I really wanted was some confirmation and felt I got that in spades. Even so, I can't say it was good to see Nick again. It saddened me to admit that, but it saddened me even more seeing what his life had become. I had never been much of a religious man, but if I were, I'd have a few blessings to count; a good upbringing, loving home and now a family of my own. But since I wasn't particularly religious, all I could do was silently thank my parents for sweeping me away from Broken Tree when they did. If there was any question before, it only took seeing Nick to realize it was absolutely the right decision.

The slamming of the car door resonated in the otherwise noiseless evening. I took my time walking up to the gate and spent it scanning the cemetery grounds through the iron bars. I took even longer to try the latch that secured the gate. It didn't budge. By all appearances, the old, rusted locking mechanism remained fully engaged. The towering barrier whose sole purpose was to keep people out of the cemetery was intent on doing just that. I shook the gate like doing so was supposed to help. All I got for my effort was the ringing out of clanging metal.

I jammed my hands into my jeans pockets and started walking along the stone and iron fence that surrounded the cemetery. The names so perfectly etched into the headstones seemed familiar, even though I couldn't have actually remembered them from all that time ago. More likely, these same common names graced the headstones in every cemetery in America: Parker, Hamilton, and Rutledge. Said together, the names sounded like a law firm. I chuckled nervously to myself, making it official; when I'm nervous, I tend to let my private thoughts devolve into jokes for no other reason than to calm and amuse myself. My nerves such as they were, it was quite possible there could be more jokes to come.

I pulled my hands from my pockets and blew hot air into them, the liquid heat from the two beers having long ago worn off. The fact that it was only October and I was already in need of gloves was something that would take some getting used to. I hadn't dressed at all for the occasion; that was bitterly obvious. So I did what I could and turned up the collar on my fleece jacket.

I'm not sure if it was my lack of preparedness that made me

consider giving up and going home, or if it was the mounting anxiety. The more time I spent in the presence of the cemetery, the more I felt I wasn't alone. And that was an unnerving feeling considering mine was the only car parked in the turnaround. Right now, heading home to the warmth of Cheryl and Ben sounded like the best plan I'd had in awhile.

But they would have to wait. There was something I needed to do first.

"Connor." Even whispering the name resulted in a breach of the stillness. Yet almost immediately, I felt the approaching of some nearby presence. Just to confirm that I was indeed on my own, I checked up and down the fence line in both directions. But as far as I could tell, no one was around to witness my little plunge into insanity. I checked the parking lot once more before...

"Connor?"

I felt dumb. Who was I even talking to? The wind? The trees? I might as well have, because I sure as hell wasn't talking to a twelve-year-old boy who'd been dead for twenty-five years, was I? With a sinking feeling creeping into my stomach, I reminded myself that was exactly who I was talking to. But at least I had a good reason...

There's a ghost in the cemetery. He's waiting for his friends.

The part of me that didn't feel quite so dumb reminded the rest of me that I did have a couple beers in me. Like somehow that would make it more acceptable, or at least justify why I was standing here trying to strike up a conversation with a ghost. Then I reminded myself that they'd been light beers and their effect on me was probably nil. Excuse gone.

I felt something tickle my upper lip. Subtle and faint, but a tickle nonetheless. I put the back of my hand to it and my hand came away slick and wet. Even in the diminishing light of the sun, I knew instantly that it was blood.

My nose was bleeding.

But, that was impossible. I hadn't had a bloody nose since I was ten-years-old. I remember it specifically because it was the only bloody nose I've had in my entire life. Things like that have a way of staying with you. Like the first time you kiss a girl. Or discover dumpster pornography with your childhood friends.

Connor and I had been playing football in the yard, and football not being all that much fun with only two people, all it took was one hard tackle for the game to devolve into a wrestling match. Kind of like "King of the Hill" minus the hill. Now with Connor being the small and frail one, and me having to wear the husky jeans from Woolworth's, it wasn't an even match. But occasionally, I got lazy and Connor would get the upper hand. One such time, Connor managed to clock me with an errant elbow.

Now, here I was, standing outside the cemetery fence with only the second nosebleed of my life, and I couldn't help but wonder if they didn't have something in common.

Connor.

A sudden breeze rustled my hair along with the few remaining leaves on the trees. Where there were no more leaves, the tree limbs swayed gently side to side, lightly clicking as their naked branches touched.

I rooted through my jacket pockets for a tissue. With the new climate, Ben's allergies had been bothering him lately, so I'd been carrying a wad with me at all times. Pulling the tissues out, I peeled one off and wiped the blood from my lip. I took another, ripped it, twisted it and packed it tightly into both nostrils. I could imagine how I looked, standing outside a cemetery, talking to a ghost with white corkscrews sticking out of my nose. I felt dumb, of that I couldn't be more certain.

"Connor?" I said, this time louder. Gripping the iron bars, I peered into the cemetery like a prisoner looking out onto a world he'd long ago given up. After a deep exhale, I took the next logical step. "Connor, I know you're there. It's Adam. I want to talk."

The cemetery trees responded instantly. Gently swaying limbs suddenly became whips, violently snapping against one another. The gusts picked leaves off the ground and tossed them about, swirling like a tornado. I'd heard the wind referred to as howling before, and that was exactly how it started to sound. It was a sorrowful howl, and its clamor grew louder with every passing second.

I never experienced anything like it. It was as if someone, or some *thing*, was growing agitated. Clouds swiftly moved in, extinguishing what little light the rising moon had been providing. I watched as shadows slowly blended, ultimately morphing into the darkness completely. Headstones, trees and clumps of overgrown shrubs all faded into the night. But one thing frightened me more than anything else to that point: everything the energy touched, all the chaotic frenzy that was ravaging the cemetery, remained imprisoned behind iron bars. Even the gusting wind seemed miraculously contained wholly within the confines of the fence. Trees perched outside the fence remained still, calm as if painted on canvas, somehow unaffected by the howling gales. And I didn't feel them either. No rush of air caressed my face. The raging energy, so fierce only steps away, remained shielded from me, and in some ways, that was more difficult to fathom than the existence of a ghost.

Devouring the scene with eager eyes, they came to rest on my car parked in the turnaround, a mere black void in the absence of light. The car beckoned me, and I wanted to comply. But I was frozen. My legs wouldn't move. The tiny hairs on the back of my neck rose and stood on end and still I remained. A shiver wracked my shoulders and it took a moment to realize it wasn't a product of the air. In fact, I wasn't even cold anymore. As I stood in forty-degree weather, little more to protect me than a thin jacket, I no longer suffered from the chill I'd felt earlier. The static electricity coursing about the air was warming my skin through my clothes.

But that wasn't all it was doing. My arms began to itch. Just a little at first, the sensation grew to the point where my skin felt like I'd been rolling in a patch of poison ivy, or had been bitten by a million hairy spiders. I struggled to ease the irritation, but I soon realized I couldn't scratch the itch away. In fact, I had to claw at my arms in order to penetrate the sleeves of my fleece jacket to get even the slightest bit of relief.

My God, it itched so bad!

"Connor! Please!"

Above the howling wind, a new sound caught my attention. A popping sound, like the snapping of a wishbone. I imagined the thousands of coffins buried below ground, their contents coming to life. The image dispatched another shiver as the racket echoed around me. Another sound, this one much louder, drew my eyes skyward. Fear soon followed.

One by one, tree limbs began plummeting from the sky, crashing to the ground and splintering into smaller pieces as they landed. All throughout the cemetery, it was raining tree limbs and branches of all sizes. The snapping eventually drowned out the wind and the sheer volume of it all became unbearable. I clamped my hands tight over my ears.

I felt the splinters hit my face before I saw what happened.

Not five feet away, a branch the length of an old Buick hit the ground just on the other side of the fence. Exploding on impact, the outburst showered me with shards of wood.

The pelting of splinters against my bare skin snapped me out of my trance, enabling me to tear myself away from the fence and the vulgar display of power taking place inside. I kicked up grass and gravel on my way to the car. It was only once I'd reached it that I risked a quick glance behind me. The scene playing out could only be described as sheer and utter carnage. And the most frightening part? I could feel it happening as much as see it. A force underscored the chaos, something akin to kinetic energy. It charged the air, and I couldn't decide if that energy was born of rage or excitement.

Throwing open the car door, I climbed behind the steering wheel and embraced the security. I'd left the key in the ignition and quickly found it with trembling hands. The headlights came on automatically, flooding the cemetery in bright light, giving birth once again to shadows. The black silhouettes of trees danced about the graveyard without any sense of choreography.

It was a mesmerizing scene. Wild with insanity and terror.

A moment later, I tore my eyes away and threw the car in reverse. Gravel pinged off the undercarriage as I pulled through the turnaround and onto the road. The tires squealed and chirped when they hit asphalt, propelling me away from the cemetery and back toward town.

Minutes later, I was safe in my driveway. Only then did I breathe easy. Crossing my arms over the steering wheel, I buried my head. And I wept. I wept like a man who'd just encountered a long lost friend he'd thought was dead. I wept like the friend who was supposed to return for him, but didn't. Mostly, and for the first time I could remember, I wept for Connor Westphal.

Chapter Ten

He sat atop the tallest tree in the graveyard and looked down at the destruction. The broken limbs. The scattered leaves. There were even a few cracked and chipped headstones littering the cemetery grounds. This was his doing, all of it, and that knowledge filled him with equal parts satisfaction and disappointment. He'd been too excited, had tried too hard, wanting his old friend to see all the power he had. His strength. Mostly, he wanted to show Adam that he wasn't a helpless twelve-year-old anymore, despite the fact that eternal childhood was his destiny.

But, he'd gone too far and it had scared Adam away. He had the strength and the power, of that there was no doubt, but lacked the will to restrain himself. In many ways, he remained very much a child. A child with tantrum-like tendencies. Still, he was confident his point had gotten across. He knew Adam would be back at some point. Knew he couldn't resist. Adam would come back, and if he had anything to do with it, Adam would never leave again.

Chapter Eleven

I was still reeling.

It had been a week and a half since the night the cemetery sprang to life, and it was still all my mind could focus on. If Cheryl had noticed, she didn't say. Like a chronic sickness, I couldn't get over the feeling the cemetery—the actual cemetery!—had wanted to harm me. Like it was literally trying to get *at* me, but couldn't reach beyond the fence.

It had been so bizarre, that at times, I wasn't even sure it really happened. But, down deep I knew that it had. Part of me wanted to drive out to the cemetery and to prove it to myself. Just to see if the grounds were still in the condition I'd left them, littered with fallen tree limbs and damaged headstones. By all appearances, a storm had blown through, leaving destruction in its wake. But, I knew that what happened that night had nothing to do with a storm. Or any other natural occurrence.

The nights that followed, the duration of my sleep could be measured in minutes instead of hours, my mind refusing to let go of that night's events. However, my body eventually got to the point it could no longer go without rest and overruled my brain. Finally, I slept. But my mind wasn't going quietly into that good night, and my sleep wasn't restful. Dreams, or rather nightmares, replayed like reels of celluloid film that seemed to have no end. After a few days, the films played with less frequency, and eventually ceased altogether. My restless mind had ultimately laid down its weapons and we called a truce.

At first, I'd considered sharing the experience with Cheryl, but ultimately decided she would do one of two things: think I was crazy and blow it off, or freak out and insist on doing something even more insane, like move back to Arizona.

And for me, admitting I was wrong and moving back wasn't an option.

Or, was it? We could cut and run and never look back. We've done it before...

Unfortunately, the voice in my head had grown louder as of late, telling me I should never have come back to Broken Tree. Should never have brought my family here. That I should have left well enough alone. I was finding it more and more difficult to tune the voice out. Doubt, guilt and pangs of regret were becoming my new best friends.

Though I still would never admit that to Cheryl.

Now, as I leaned against the car, gasoline chugging through the pump, I had something altogether different occupying my thoughts. Something much more pleasant and welcome. Something that pointed toward the future instead of the past.

We'd been in the auditorium at Ben's school taking in his Fall program. It was the kind of performance only a parent could enjoy. It had all the usual suspects: the off-key singing, the bad acting and a stage set that said, "we spent most of our budget on the cookies and punch that will immediately follow." Suffice to say, we were enjoying the hell out of it all. Ben had been cast as a farmer and dressed the part in full denim overalls, red and black flannel shirt and brown knobby-soled boots, all of which we'd found at a Goodwill store. The red bandana around his neck he'd borrowed from Cheryl, whose mother's pride was evident by the smile that never left her face.

Then, as Ben sang about the harvest with a trio of other fourth grade farmers, Cheryl leaned over and whispered in my ear. Once her carefully chosen words had been spoken, she nonchalantly straightened back in her seat and returned her attention to the program. She was cool and calm, acting as if she had just given me the weather report instead of the biggest news since the move. I, on the other hand, could do nothing but turn and stare at her in awe. Not to mention a little disbelief.

I want to have another child.

Six simple words, spoken out of the blue, had me falling in love with my wife all over again. Cheryl must have felt my stare, because she turned and met my eyes, a sparkle in hers. *Are you sure?* I simply mouthed the words and her smile grew by at least a third before she turned back to the kids on the stage. But, that was all the answer I needed. We had a lot to discuss once we got home, and I couldn't wait to get back and put Ben to bed.

I leaned against the car, gas pump still chugging away, and looked up at the night sky. Even without big city lights to wash out the stars, few were visible. Scattered stretches of clouds were passing through. The moon was playing a creepy version of peek-a-boo behind their cloak, and no matter how hard I tried, I couldn't make out the man who supposedly lived in it. Never had been able to, in fact, even though I'd always heard the phrase growing up.

Ben was turned sideways in the backseat making faces at me through the window. At one point, his nose was pressed so hard against the glass that it made mine hurt. But the more he tried to get my attention, the more I pretended not to notice. It was a fun game, one we played often, and it was all I could do to keep from laughing.

Inside the gas station, Cheryl hovered in front of the cooler case, trying to decide which orange juice to get for breakfast in the morning. Lately, low-pulp and organic had been playing tug of war with her; organic for her health conscious side, low-pulp for the taste. I was rooting for the latter.

I had turned to make a face back at Ben when I noticed the reflection of a man behind me in the darkened window. I immediately tensed up as he approached. Having lived in the city for many years, being approached by a stranger at a gas station at night was never a good thing in my experience. What I found when I turned toward him, however, was less a threat than an inconvenience. And less of a man than a drunken, disheveled remnant of one. Nick Gant had stumbled up and was now leaning against the pump.

My heart sank.

"I know you." He'd gotten right to the point. Usually, I respected that in a person. Usually. I looked up and down the street trying to figure out where the hell he'd come from.

"I'm sorry?"

He swayed as if a gust of wind had gotten hold of him, but I didn't feel anything. "I know who you are."

I peered nervously into the store. I could see Cheryl standing in line behind what looked to be at least one other person. I had a minute, maybe two to get rid of Nick before she came out and started asking questions.

"Look, buddy," I said, reaching into my back pocket for my wallet, "need a couple bucks or something?"

"I don't need your goddamn money." Nick hacked up a wad of phlegm and spat it onto the ground between our feet, turning my stomach.

Straining against my revulsion, I pulled a five and a few ones from my wallet and thrust them in Nick's direction. It was all I had on me, and I hoped like hell it would be enough to buy his silence, or at least get him to walk away. He eyed the money for a second, as if weighing its worth against his agenda, then shook his head. He looked away in disgust, like he couldn't believe he was turning it down.

"I'm goin' out there," he said. Agitation mixed with a healthy dose of determination had settled into his voice.

"Out where?" I'd asked the question having already known the answer. It didn't take a rocket scientist to figure out where "out there" was in the context of this conversation.

"The cemetery." But instead of looking at me like I was stupid, Nick simply wiped his nose with his sleeve. "He's still out there, ya know? He's still waiting. For us."

"Us?" My heart rate escalated at the inclusion. Looking for Cheryl, I found her at the register now. It wouldn't be long. In turning back around, I caught a glimpse of Ben in the back seat, face still pressed against the glass, only his expression was no longer playful. Concern wasn't generally an expression I liked seeing on my nine-year-old. I tried conjuring up a reassuring smile, but it came off more like, "I apologize in advance for anything bad that may come from this."

"Me and you, Adam," Nick said. "Connor's still waiting for me and you to find him."

My jaw dropped at the sound of my name. There was no longer any doubt that Nick knew who I was. This wasn't going to make living in Broken Tree any easier from this moment forward.

"Look, pal, I don't know what you're talking about, but—"

"Jesus Christ, Adam!" He spat the words at me like so much sputum. "Are you coming with me or not?"

I searched for the right words. The only clarity I experienced was the idea that further attempts at maintaining anonymity would be futile. So I gave up the charade, took a deep breath and simply answered his question.

"No, Nick, I'm not. And I wouldn't recommend you go out there either. It's dangerous."

His eyes lit up. "So you believe me." It was more a statement than a question.

"Yes," I said, feeling strange admitting it out loud. "I believe you. I believe in something, at least. But, I'm asking you to turn around and walk away. For good. From me *and* the cemetery."

Nick's eyes narrowed as he judged my suggestion. Slowly his head started nodding up and down. A grin drew back the corners of his mouth and creased the whiskers on his face that were in the process of turning grey.

"You've been there."

I shook my head. "Seriously, Nick." I could feel my voice rising and I fought to wrestle it back into submission. "I don't know what's going on out there, okay? I don't. But I suggest you go home and forget all about—"

"Honey?"

My heart sank at the sound of Cheryl's voice. An unfamiliar sensation, for sure. I followed Nick's eyes and turned to find we had an audience. Cheryl stood at the front of the car holding a plastic bag large enough to bear two different kinds of orange juice.

"Everything alright?" Concern painted her face like oils on a canvas.

"Yeah, we're good." I offered what I was sure was another weak smile. It wasn't a lie; I had the situation under control. She wasn't dismissed easily, but my smile must have been reassuring enough to ease at least some of her anxiety. She finally relented and made her way to the passenger side, but not before shifting her eyes back and forth between the strange man and me. Once I heard her door close, I turned my attention back to Nick, hoping like hell he'd be gone.

He wasn't.

Nick remained where he was, still expecting an answer that I was pretty sure I had already given. Apparently it hadn't been the right one.

"I'm not going, Nick," I said, doing my best to put my foot down with the tone of my voice. "I'm sorry, but I'm taking my family home and that's exactly where you should go. Then, you should forget all about that cemetery and whatever may or may not be there."

The latch holding the gas nozzle open clicked off. *Thank God.* I jiggled the handle, pulled it from the car's gas tank and hung it back on the pump. As I waited impatiently for the receipt, the seconds gathered like flies on a pile of shit. It was taking unusually longer than normal for the machine to spit out the receipt. *Come on!* But the little slip of paper never showed. Instead, the words "see attendant" scrolled across the screen.

"Screw it." Instead of going into the gas station to ask for a copy of the receipt, I ignored the suggestion and simply headed toward the front of the car. I wasn't spending a second longer at the gas station than necessary.

Nick watched in silence as I walked away.

Before opening my door, I shot one last glance in his direction. "Go home, Nick."

But he simply looked at me with an awkward grin and nodded. "I'll tell him you said hello."

As I got in the car and started it up, I could feel two sets of eyes on me. I met one of them, and Cheryl offered me a weak smile. On my way back to the car, I had already started compiling a list of answers to the questions I thought for sure were coming: he was a homeless man looking for a handout; he was lost and needed directions; he was looking for his Shih Tzu that had gotten off her leash. But something in Cheryl's smile told me she already knew the truth.

"Was that man homeless, Dad?"

I didn't even have to think about my answer. "Nah, Bennie, he wasn't." And I put the car in gear.

Then, from the backseat, "He looked homeless."

I decided to let it go for now and simply smiled at my son in the rearview mirror. Behind him, Nick Gant still leaned against the pump, watching us pull away. He didn't disappear until falling victim to distance, and the shameful side of me, the side you shield from others and barely acknowledge yourself, hoped like hell I'd never see him again.

Chapter Twelve

The following day was uncharacteristically Spring-like, considering the weather Minnesota traditionally sees in mid-October. That afternoon, the sky was filled with more blue than clouds and the mercury hovered in the low seventies. All over Broken Tree, people were out and about, taking the opportunity to squeeze in another jog or give the dog one more walk before cold weather hit. We took advantage of the gracious weather by planning a picnic in the park. Actually, Cheryl planned it; I just loaded the car. It was a rarity for the Bishop family, even though we were always saying we needed to spend more time outside. Unfortunately, living in the Southwest makes it all too easy to turn into an "indoors person." Something I really hoped to change now that we were out from under Arizona's oppressive heat.

On the lunch menu were turkey sandwiches, chips, string cheese, grapes, Cheryl's famous oatmeal raisin cookies and a thermos of sweet tea to wash it all down. I'd also thrown Ben's soccer ball and the biggest blanket we had into the car. The only picnic staple we didn't have were the customary ants, and I was feeling so good, I probably would have welcomed them had they shown up.

After the food was gone and our bellies full, Cheryl kicked back on the blanket with a new romance paperback, and Ben and I took to a nearby open space to kick the soccer ball around. Like snow shoes and colorful toboggans, soccer was another thing you didn't see much of in Arizona, yet was plentiful in Minnesota. Everywhere you looked around town, kids were kicking soccer balls, and it hadn't taken long for Ben to develop an interest. Several of his new friends played on teams, something Ben hinted at giving a try. Having played myself when I was his age, I immediately wanted to bestow upon my son some of my limited soccer knowledge. At least that which I could remember.

"If you kick with the inside of your foot," I said, "you can control the ball better." Along with a bit of technique that more than one coach had taught me, I passed the ball to Ben, who trapped it just like I'd shown him minutes earlier. Then, after positioning the ball where he wanted, he returned it using the inside of his foot.

"See? Perfect." Ben was obviously a natural. At least in my opinion, which may or may not be biased. Pretty sure I wouldn't be the first father to think his child would grow up to be the next superstar with their own line of shoes. There would be plenty of fathers in that team picture, each quietly wishing a sprained ankle to befall the other kids. We wouldn't be proud of it, but that wouldn't make it untrue.

We kicked the ball back and forth a few more times, each pass from Ben more perfect than the last. But while I couldn't have been more content, spending such a beautiful day at the park with my son, the look on Ben's face told me he was growing bored with the menial exercise of simply passing back and forth. Even though his passing was improving with each kick, there was also less enthusiasm behind each one. About the time I expected him to start complaining, a blonde-haired boy roughly Ben's age jogged up beside him.

The boys chatted while Ben and I continued passing the ball.

As hard as I strained, I couldn't hear their conversation, but the fact that there was a fair amount of giggling involved made me paranoid. I couldn't help but wonder if I was the source of their humor. Surely we hadn't already reached that point where Ben was embarrassed to be hanging out with his old man, had we? I hoped not. He was only nine after all. But, each subsequent generation did seem to grow up faster than the last.

Thankfully, my paranoia proved unwarranted when Ben's friend joined in and started kicking the ball with us. Though it wasn't long before I started receiving less of Ben's attention with most of the conversations taking place between the two boys. However, I will admit to it being nice seeing Ben interact with someone his own age. Cheryl and I had worried about his adjustment to a new town and school, whether or not he'd have difficulty making new friends. But from where I stood, it looked like Ben was doing just fine. He obviously took after his mother in that regard.

Eventually, it became so embarrassingly apparent that I was the third wheel, I quietly excused myself to join Cheryl on the blanket.

"Any good?"

"Huh?" Both her eyes and attention remained on the book.

Laying down beside her on the blanket, I propped myself up on my elbow and tapped the book's cover. On it was a man with a long flowing mane and an outfit that hadn't made it out of the 19th century. "Is it any good?"

"Not bad," Cheryl said. "It's a little slow in places, but the hot parts are definitely five alarm." She made no attempt to conceal her smile.

"Really?" I cozied up to her. "Is it putting you in the mood for anything? Anything at all?" I ran my hand over her hip, expecting her to pull away. I was pleasantly surprised when she didn't. Public displays of affection had become hit and miss with Cheryl.

"Why, Mr. Bishop," she said, in her sweetest, most innocent voice, "what on Earth could you have in mind?"

If the fact that she didn't pull away had surprised me, that she was actually playing along caught me completely off guard. I found myself ill-prepared with an answer. It's not like we *never* talked flirtatiously. In fact, before Ben came along, we were the couple that embarrassed our friends with our flirting. Instances such as this had simply become exceedingly rare since the miscarriage. It's funny how talks of having another child can affect a relationship. Opening the dam gates, even a crack, allows the water to flow more freely, I guess.

I answered Cheryl's question the only way I knew how: with a kiss on her shoulder. Then her neck. I was about to move on to her earlobe when...

"Dad! Mom!" I hadn't heard Ben approach, but here he was, throwing cold water on any heat I may have generated in the last few minutes. It was just as well. We were in a public park, after all. The last thing either of us wanted was to be that inappropriate couple parents shielded their children's eyes from.

"What?" Cheryl and I responded in unison, experiencing the same level of alarm.

"Devin's leaving and he asked his mom if I could go home with them and hang out and play stuff and have dinner and—"

"Whoa, Bennie," Cheryl said, shrugging me off and getting to her feet. "Slow down. I can't keep up, honey. First thing's first, what's your friend's name?"

"Devin."

I could tell by the way he shifted his weight back and forth that Ben was struggling to contain his excitement. Either that, or he had to pee really badly. Poor kid, either way.

"And he's going home?" she said.

Ben's nod came rapidly, his anxious smile never faltering.

"And basically, you're asking if you can go with him."

"Yes! Please?"

Cheryl frowned, then looked down at me.

"I don't know," she said, her voice thick with apprehension. It wasn't that Cheryl was overprotective or overbearing. She was just naturally cautious. "We don't even know Devin. Or his parents."

I glanced over at the parking lot where a woman was busy loading a cooler into the back of a grey minivan. She looked to be about our age and pleasant enough. Ben's friend stood beside her and they both waved when they saw me looking their way.

Rising behind Cheryl, I put my hands on her hips and leaned in close to her ear. "You know, we'd have the house to ourselves." I'd started nibbling on her earlobe when she turned and met my gaze. Fantastically, that's all it took. Within a matter of a few seconds, she had bought what I was selling and her bashful smile told me we were on the same page.

"Come on, Bennie," I said, taking my son's hand. "Let's go meet Devin's mom."

Halfway to the parking lot, I shot a glance back at Cheryl. She wasn't wasting any time. Empty food containers were already packed into the basket and she was hurriedly folding the blanket.

Chapter Thirteen

"Turn right, one hundred feet." The voice giving instruction was less than personable. In fact, I hated it. Apparently I could go online and download any number of impersonated celebrity voices to use with my GPS, but I only ever thought about it while in the car and without Wi-Fi. I was thinking Christopher Walken or Sean Connery would be a welcome change. Either would be better than the monotone robotic voice it came with. Hell, even a droll Alan Rickman would be an improvement.

I realized while on my way to pick up Ben, just how handy a GPS app for your phone was. My mind wasn't exactly focused at the moment, and I wouldn't have wanted to depend on my navigational skills. I was still basking in the glow of a rare afternoon lovemaking session. Saying my mind was elsewhere was like saying the upcoming Minnesota winter would be quite the adjustment for a family from Arizona. Without the less than personable voice telling me what to do, there's no telling where I'd end up.

"Turn right. Iroquois Street."

The passion was back. Whether it was the recent talk of having another baby that fueled it, or the dam we'd subconsciously erected over the last few years had given way, unable to hold the passion any longer. Either way, we'd made love that afternoon like we hadn't since Ben was born. Our kisses were deeper than I remembered. Our touches, electric. The climaxes were of the kind written about in the books Cheryl read, the kind most real people only dreamed about. And the absolute best thing about the entire event? Cheryl hadn't stopped me at any point in the process, asking me to put on a condom. Apparently, the discussions we'd been having lately weren't just lip service. She was truly ready to board the baby train again after such a long wait. We were at least headed in the right direction.

And I would have hated to see what would have happened to all that intense passion had I needed to stop and make an impromptu run to the pharmacy.

"Turn left, Azalea Avenue. Your destination is one hundred and fifty feet ahead."

Something in my mind clicked. Up to that point, I'd blindly followed the directions being given me. Turning left when the GPS said to turn left. Turning right when it said to turn right. Following the road dead ahead the rest of the time. It wasn't until I heard the words "Azalea Avenue" that my attention snapped to my whereabouts.

The cemetery.

It was on Route 36. Otherwise known as Azalea Avenue.

I felt a sudden hitch in my throat. The name of the street hadn't even registered when I put the address into the GPS. I'd been so consumed with—

My stomach lurched at the seriousness of my mistake.

*   *   *

It glowed a soft orange in the fading light of evening. I pushed the button beside the door and heard a chime signal inside the house. After waiting only a few seconds, I abruptly pushed the button a second time. Then, much sooner than deemed polite, I skipped the doorbell altogether and rapped my knuckles on the wooden door with the decorative glass insert. My heart was beating fast, too fast in fact, but I couldn't blame it at this point. I could only hope that my anxiety had no merit.

I stood on the porch of the last house on the street and looked out over the adjoining field to the cemetery a half mile away. Just knowing my son was this close to the dreaded place was enough to fill me with torment. Different than the concern you feel when sending a child off to their first day of kindergarten, and worse than sitting with them in an emergency room with a temperature well above one hundred. What I felt was different than anything I was accustomed to.

This was pure, unadulterated fear.

Just as I'd raised my fist to knock once again, a shadow passed by the glass insert and the door opened. Devin's mother, whose name I'd learned earlier was Constance, greeted me with an awkward smile and a half-cocked look of annoyance.

"Hi, Constance," I said, "I'm here to pick up Ben. Is he ready?" No time for small talk. I couldn't get my son the hell out of that neighborhood fast enough.

"Hi…Adam, right? I'm sorry, but the boys aren't back yet."

An alarm sounded in my head before I knew there was even cause for it.

"I'm sorry?" I said. "Back from where?"

"Oh, you know boys. Always looking for adventure." She smiled, as if that would soften the blow from what was coming next. "They went down the road to do a little ghost hunting. They were supposed to be home a half hour—"

I was already off the porch, taking the steps two at a time. I wasn't sure of everything she'd said, having heard nothing beyond the word "ghost." Nothing, that is, except my brain screaming.

I jerked up on the driver's side door handle and flopped into the seat. I had the car running and in gear before remembering to shut the door. I was certain Constance thought I was either incredibly rude or savagely insane. If not a touch of both. But I couldn't worry about that right now. I had to reach Ben...

Before Connor did.

"Shit!" I said, slapping my palm on the steering wheel. Thoughts of Connor right then were premature, I knew. But I couldn't deny they existed. I should have never let Ben go with his friend. I should have kept him close and in my care. But, how could I have known where his friend lived? Because she told you, that's how. Standing in the parking lot, I'd never even asked where they lived. I'd simply handed over my phone so that Devin's mom could enter it directly. *Azalea Avenue!* I'd been too damn preoccupied with the prospects of an afternoon alone with Cheryl to think about anything else. But that was no defense.

With dusk quickly giving way to night, I was having trouble seeing the road, despite the aid of headlights. It didn't help that my head swirled with emotion and I allowed my eyes to stray from the road. The car went straight on a slight curve, kicking up gravel from the berm. I wrenched the steering wheel to the left and pressed harder on the gas pedal. Only a steep incline stood between the cemetery and me.

Between Ben and me.

My God, what would we do if we lost him? I hated myself for even allowing the thought into my head, but now that the question was there, it begged to be answered. Would Cheryl be able to cope with the loss? I wasn't sure I would be able to. In fact, given the circumstances, I knew I wouldn't. In the barest of realities, if something were to happen in that cemetery, it would be my fault. Without question. His death would serve as penance for something I'd done many years ago. Or *not* done. Might as well lay down in the cemetery and start shoveling the dirt over myself.

I crested the hill at a rate of speed beyond that which I would normally feel comfortable. But I wasn't deterred. My hands ached from gripping the steering wheel so tight, but I dared not loosen my grip. Not only was it better than seeing my hands tremble, but I was having trouble controlling the car under that speed as it was. I was fighting to keep it between the yellow centerline and the gravel berm.

"Stay on the asphalt," I beseeched the car. "Stay on the road."

They were in front of me before I even realized it. Two young boys, Devin and Ben, walking along the side of the road. Walking right toward me. My heart dropped into my stomach. I was pretty sure I stopped breathing.

The boys shielded their eyes from the oncoming headlights.

I cut the wheel hard to the left. I stomped both feet on the brake pedal. As the car swerved, its rear end swung around. For a fraction of a second, I met Ben's eyes. They were wide with fear. Then just as quickly, the boys were out of my line of sight as the car continued its fishtail. I felt a solid hitch from the rear and let out a cry.

No! God, no!

The car skidded to a stop. The screeching of rubber rivaled the screaming taking place in my head. I was in the opposite lane, facing a full one hundred and eighty degrees from where I'd been heading only a moment earlier. The town now lay out in front of me, the cemetery behind.

It had all happened in the time it takes a freight train to turn a stalled car into something that no longer resembles its former self.

So damn quick.

And Ben was dead, I just knew it.

I slammed the car into park and threw open the door all in one motion. Jumping out, I spun in the direction I'd last seen the boys. Bracing myself, I expected there to be blood splayed across the road, a small, crumpled body lying in the middle of it. Maybe two.

But, there was nothing. No blood. No body. Only fresh skid marks scarring the faded asphalt.

"Ben!" I began searching frantically, at a loss as to where my son might be. I looked all around the car, even underneath. *God, no!* I looked in both the pool of the headlights as well as the shadows. But he was nowhere.

Then, I heard two small and distant voices. I stopped cold and tried to triangulate where those voices were coming from. Steadily, the voices edged louder. When I realized they were coming from behind me, I did a one-eighty and took a few steps in that direction. Rising from the ditch that ran beside the road were two small hands.

The boys looked scared, but were otherwise alive and uninjured. At least at first glance. I ran over, meeting them on the edge of the road. Before either of us could say a word, I dropped to my knees and swept Ben up in my arms. Hugging him tighter than I probably ever had, I felt the distinct sensation of tears running down my cheeks.

Once I could finally separate myself from Ben, the father in me began checking him for cuts or scrapes. Thankfully, other than fresh grass stains on his jeans and a little mud on his jacket, he was fine and repeatedly told me so. When I realized the bump I'd felt was probably the tires skidding across the asphalt, I was more than relieved. I was liberated.

With the crisis averted, I let go of the fact I had almost killed my only son and addressed the reason we were in this situation in the first place.

"Don't you ever go into that cemetery again, do you understand me?" I had him by the shoulders, and it was all I could do to keep from shaking him, my fear turning to anger. "Do you understand me, Ben? Never! It's not safe!"

"We're fine, Dad!" Ben cried, the terror in his eyes more pronounced at my outburst than when faced with the prospect of being run over. "We didn't even go inside!"

"I don't care!" I was shouting, completely ignoring the look of shock on both boys' faces. "That cemetery is not a place for children to play, and I don't ever want to hear about you going in there again!"

Ben's eyes were so wide there was nothing to stop the tears. It was the streams that started trailing down his cheeks more than anything that broke my anger. That's when I moved on to the third stage of emotion in a matter of minutes: regret.

It was true. Ben and his friend hadn't done anything wrong. I never instructed him *not* to go into the cemetery. I never told him how unsafe it could be. It was my own fear that had almost cost me my one and only child.

My anger nearly drained, I embraced Ben once more before putting him in the car and taking him home.

Chapter Fourteen

He stood at the gate, looking through the iron bars to the road beyond. The fact that he could no longer see the boys saddened him. An opportunity missed. Children almost never came to the cemetery anymore, much less alone, and he had barely been able to contain himself at the possibilities.

Two things had stood in his way. The first being that the boys hadn't climbed the fence and actually entered the cemetery. Hadn't even tried. The second thing that stood in his way, and this had caught him off guard, was the familiarity of one of the boys. He wasn't sure what it was about the small, dark-haired boy, but it stirred something deep within him. A feeling. A memory. And for that reason alone, he'd chosen to hang back and observe instead of drawing them in.

But, now he stood here, still alone. He could feel his sadness slowly turning to anger. It was an all too familiar sensation, and when he was angry, he thought of only two things: Nick Gant and Adam Bishop, and how they should be here with him.

The trees around him started to wave, birds scattered. And he swore that he'd never let another opportunity pass him by.

Chapter Fifteen

One problem you encounter when moving from Arizona to Minnesota is that you tend not to bring a box marked "winter clothes." And in Minnesota, winter is no joke and seasonal clothing is a must. In Arizona, you covet the small patches of grass interspersed with all the sand. Treasure and manicure them due to their rarity. Minnesota, on the other hand, has plenty of grass. It's everywhere. Only problem is, you can go months without seeing any due to the inches, and sometimes feet, of billowy white snow. *Might as well embrace it,* my coworkers have told me. *It's coming regardless.*

So while Cheryl covered a rare Sunday shift for a co-worker, I decided to get Ben out of the house and go shopping for his inaugural winter coat. Lately, we'd spent a lot more time inside than we'd wanted, and it had little to do with the changing weather. Being at home just felt safer. But, it had been over a week since I nearly ran Ben over with the car. It was time to put it behind us and move on with our lives. Get back on the old horse, as they say.

After finding little of interest at the first two department stores, we'd come away without a coat for Ben, but not completely empty-handed. We were the proud owners of a pair of wool-lined leather gloves for myself, and a couple packs of Halo trading cards for Ben. I had the energy to try one more store. If our luck in finding Ben a coat didn't improve, well then, the search would have to be postponed until I could enlist Cheryl's help.

After a much needed break to fill up on chicken wings and the first half of the Viking game down at Matty's, we found ourselves in the boy's department of the recently opened Target store. While Ben grumbled his way through the selection of boy's coats, I caught myself prematurely checking out the tiny coats in the *really* little kid's section. They looked no bigger than doll's clothes.

The thought both excited and terrified me.

Other than Ben and me, there was one other person sorting through the winter coats. A woman, who I would estimate was in her early sixties and possessing a name like Mabel, had her hair wrapped in a bright orange scarf. But the scarf wasn't what caught my attention. It was the salacious smile she wore that said 'my husband won't be home for a couple hours.' I ignored her the best I could, concentrating on finding Ben a coat, but the couple times our eyes happened to meet made me uncomfortable. Thankfully, another woman approached Mabel before I found myself in the unenviable position of outright shooting down an older woman's advances.

"Why hello, 'Lizabeth," I heard Mabel say before allowing the rest of their conversation to fade from my conscience. It was a relief having the woman's focus taken off me and allowed me to continue my game with Ben: I would hold up a coat and he would wrinkle his nose. Soon, Mabel and her friend couldn't have been further from my mind had they been on the other side of the store.

It was mention of the word 'cemetery,' however, that brought my attention back a few minutes later.

"I heard. Isn't it horrible?" the friend said, hand to her chest.

"And to find him in that condition..."

"I know," Mabel replied. "And it's not the first time they've found a dead body in there. Above ground, at least."

"And by 'dead,' I assume you're putting it mildly."

"Excuse me." I had no shame butting my way into their conversation. "Couldn't help overhear, something about a cemetery. Do you know what happened?"

"Oh, yes!" exclaimed the friend. "A body was found in the old cemetery out on 36 the other night. Gruesome scene."

I felt my hands clam up, and slid them into the pockets of my jacket.

"That's the second one, you know?"

"Do they know who it was?" I asked, tempering my anxiousness. "The body, I mean."

"Oh, yes," chimed Mabel. "His name was Nick Gant."

If either of the women saw the blood drain from my face, they didn't show it.

"Ben," I said, trying to keep my voice level. "Run over there to the shoes and see if you can find you a cool pair of snow boots."

"But, Mom said she was getting me a pair."

"Ben, just go. Please." He wasn't happy about it, but I watched him slink away and shuffle toward the shoes before returning my attention to the two ladies.

"What happened?" I braced myself, unsure my stomach could handle what Mabel was about to tell me.

According to the lady with the orange scarf, whom I found out wasn't named Mabel, but entirely credible due to the fact her husband was the sheriff of Broken Tree, Nick's body had been found just inside the cemetery. It lacked arms, but the rest of Nick was located about fifteen feet from the gate. His arms were actually the first part of him to be found, hanging limply from the gate itself, ripped clean at the shoulders. His frozen hands still clutched the iron bars as if he had been holding on for dear life. According to what her husband had told her, it looked like someone, or some*thing*, had been pulling on Nick as he held onto the gate, his arms having simply given way. Despite the obvious signs of trauma, the initial cause of death was being speculated as suffocation due to an abdominal amount of compression around his midsection. At least that's what all the signs pointed to. The official autopsy results wouldn't be back for a couple weeks. But the bloodshot eyes, the bruising around the abdomen. To my ears, it sounded as if Nick had been hugged to death. And I knew of only one person who could have wanted to embrace him that much.

Connor.

These graphic details must not have been shared through the usual gossip channels, because the entire time the women conversed, the friend stood aghast with one hand clutching her bosom and the other hand over her mouth. With a tremble in her voice, she muttered something about needing to move along. The two women hugged, said their goodbyes and the friend pushed her cart down the aisle and disappeared.

After the unseemly conversation, the woman with the orange scarf was understandably and thankfully done flirting. She wished me a good day, then turned away, leaving me alone with my thoughts. And right now, those thoughts were swirling in my head like miniature cows caught up in a tornado.

"That was gross."

The familiar voice came from behind me. With my heart in my throat, I turned and looked down into the scrunched up face of my nine-year-old son.

"What was?" I asked, afraid I already knew the answer.

"What that lady said about that man's body."

"Ben! How could you have heard that all the way over in the shoes?"

But, he didn't have to answer. The truth was obvious by the look on his face and the angle at which his head hung, eyes on his feet. He looked like a puppy that'd been caught digging through the trash.

"Jesus, Ben." A cold ball of lead formed in my gut as the hushed conversation with the women played back in my head, and I realized the horrific details my son had overheard. The damage was already done, I told myself. I'd only make matters worse by ignoring the situation.

"Come on," I said, hanging up the red ski coat I'd been holding. "I'm not seeing anything here. We'll wait until your mom can give us a hand."

Moments later, we were almost to the car when I instructed Ben to hop in the front seat.

"Seriously?" he asked, his excitement instantaneous. "I get to ride up front?" It was amazing how a child's mind could shift from one emotion to the next, turning on a dime. I envied that ability.

"Not exactly. Just wanna talk to ya for a minute."

Once in the car, I immediately started it up and turned on the heater. Rubbing my hands together to break the chill. Out of the corner of my eye, I noticed I had a shadow. Ben was also rubbing his hands in front of the vent. When I turned my attention to him fully, I'd already mocked up my speech while on the way to the car. I wasn't surprised that Ben beat me to the punch.

"Did the ghost get him, Dad?"

I might as well have rolled down the window and thrown my

entire speech out into the cold afternoon air. With the first words out of his mouth, Ben had sent the conversation down a different path than the one I'd planned on taking. I was caught off guard at the mention of the ghost. Ill-prepared. As much as I hated myself for doing it, I offered up the same lie that my parents always gave me.

"I don't think so, Ben," I said, swallowing my integrity, despite the necessity to. "It was an accident. A very tragic accident. Do you know what that word means? Tragic?"

Ben wrinkled up his nose and looked at me with his head cocked to one side.

"Something really bad?"

"Sort of. It means something that should have never happened or didn't need to. Something that makes people really sad."

"Are we sad that man died?"

"Yes, Ben," I said, without having to think. "It's sad anytime a person dies. Especially under circumstances like that."

He thought about it for a moment, and I could see his wheels turning as he processed.

"That lady didn't seem sad," he said a moment later. Then, after contemplating his words further, he added, "She said he was just an old drunk anyway."

I felt my heart constrict as I realized an ugly truth. That was exactly how people around town would remember Nick Gant. That is, if they remembered him at all. An old drunk.

"He wasn't always like that, Bennie." As I felt the first tear sting my eyes, I struggled to keep my voice from cracking. "He was a little boy once, too. A very good, very innocent boy."

"Like me?"

I barely got the words passed the growing lump in my throat.

"Yes, Ben. Just like you."

I managed to compose myself while Ben climbed into the back seat and buckled himself in. Seeing his old man cry shook him a little, I could tell. He didn't understand it, I'm sure. Didn't understand why was his father was shedding tears over the death of a complete stranger.

We spent the ride home in silence. Whenever I looked up in the rearview mirror, Ben would already be looking at me and our eyes would meet. There was pity in his eyes, and for the second time in days, I made Ben promise to never step foot in that cemetery. This time, and thank God for it, I was pretty sure he got the message.

Chapter Sixteen

I had barely touched my pasta. Well, that wasn't completely true. I'd spent quite a bit of time twirling it on my fork, I simply hadn't put any in my mouth. I'd twirl it until the spaghetti would be wound so tight the sauce would ooze out from between the noodles like blood through intestines in a third-rate horror movie. By then the mass of pasta was usually more than I could fit in my mouth anyway, so I'd lift my fork out of the middle of the mound and watch it collapse, waiting to be twirled again.

But, I couldn't eat.

We had finally found Ben a coat. Or, I should say, Cheryl found him a coat. She'd met us at home later that afternoon and dragged us back out to yet another store. And wielding that power only a mother possesses, found a coat Ben liked within minutes. In fact, Ben fell in love with the first one she showed him. It was like he was suddenly caught in a blizzard and needed a wool-lined protective layer right then and there. To be honest, I wasn't sure if he really liked the coat, or if he'd simply had enough shopping for one day. Either way, the task was complete and we could move on with our lives.

On the way home, we had stopped for dinner at Palmero's, a little family-owned Italian restaurant we'd discovered shortly after getting into town. It was your typical Italian joint like you see in the gangster movies with red and white-checkered tablecloths, antique tables and chairs, and signs on the walls in the shape of Italy that offered life-affirming quotes attributed to Mama Palmero. Ben was a big fan of their meatballs and Cheryl was finally getting the shrimp Alfredo she'd been craving all week. The food smelled great, as usual. I could attest to that at least.

I just couldn't eat.

I knew what I had to do, and that knowledge wasn't having a positive effect on my appetite.

The car ride home was quiet. It had been a long day, and I think Ben with his little belly full of carbs was fighting off sleep. Beside me, Cheryl was fully engrossed in a new game she'd recently downloaded onto her phone. I for one, had a lot on my mind and welcomed the downtime to think. I reached up, turned the volume on the radio a little higher so as to discourage conversation should the urge strike someone, and allowed the strips of passing yellow lines to hypnotize me.

It had already taken a year of therapy to help deal with Connor's death. Now Nick was dead, and once again, I felt responsible. I should have gone with him. Or, at least put more effort into talking him out of going. But, I'd blown him off too readily, was too eager to wash my hands of him. *And why?* Because others around town thought him strange? Usually there are very real reasons why someone acts the way they do, even when those actions fall slightly outside society's norms. And Nick had reasons aplenty for acting the way he did, living the life he'd lived. More than most people in Broken Tree knew.

But, it was too late to help Nick now.

Nick was dead.

Pulling into our driveway, I parked the car beside Cheryl's Mountaineer. I had barely shut the car off when Ben hopped out and made a beeline toward the house.

"Bennie, hold up," I called out. He stopped abruptly, dropping his shoulders and tilting his head back in defeat. I caught up with him and dropped to a knee, bringing myself to his level.

"Hey, buddy," I said, putting my hands on his shoulders and peering deep into his eyes. "Sorry I've been acting kinda weird this evening. Just got a lot on my mind."

"Like the man they found in the cemetery?" His innocent eyes searched mine, anticipating a ready-made answer.

"Partly," I offered. "Other things, too. Grown up things. Nothing you need to worry about, okay?"

He nodded and we remained there for a moment, not saying anything. Then, fighting back the tremor that threatened to work my lip, I pulled him in for a hug. A big hug. One he would remember for a very long time. I held him like that until Cheryl's hand came to rest on my shoulder.

"Ben, why don't you run on in and start your bath," she said. "I'll be up in a minute, okay?"

"Okay," he said. Pulling himself free of my arms, Ben kissed me on the forehead and ran toward the house.

I stayed low for a moment, gathering my composure, then rose as Ben leapt onto the front porch.

"Hey, Ben." I caught him just before he disappeared through the front door.

"Yeah?"

"Love you."

"Love you, too, Dad."

And then he was gone. I watched the spot where he'd stood for a few seconds, drowning in the wave of everything I wanted to tell him. How girls were to be cherished and respected. How trust, once lost, can never be fully restored. How life's truly important decisions should never be made with money in mind. All of the wisdom fathers were supposed to impart to their sons over time, I wanted to tell him right then and there.

Just in case.

Cheryl came around to face me, brushed aside my bangs with her hand. A high level of concern registered on her face, somewhere shy of outright worry. Cheryl knew me better than anyone. She was bound to pick up on the fact that I'd been dealing with something. And not just any old something. Something big.

"You okay?"

I nodded. "Just a little tired. Not feeling too well. Might be coming down with something."

Cheryl continued to search my eyes, and I doubted she was buying the "coming down with something" excuse. She was about to say something when I cut her off.

"Think I'm gonna run to the pharmacy," I said, pulling the keys from my pocket. "Need anything?"

She looked at me for another moment, her words possibly forgotten. Then, without saying anything, Cheryl leaned in like Ben had done a minute before and kissed me on the forehead. But she didn't stop there. Cheryl planted kisses all the way down my cheek and stopped only when her lips were at my ear. She hovered there for a few seconds, undoubtedly running through a list of reasons why I shouldn't go, why I should go inside with her and Ben. In the end, she resorted to none of them.

"Don't be gone long," she whispered. Then, after giving me a long kiss on the mouth, she turned away and headed up the steps to the front porch.

Chapter Seventeen

Sitting behind the wheel, staring up at the iron gate, I felt like I'd been there before. I could only hope this visit went better than the last. It could definitely go worse, but I was trying not to think about that. At least this time would be better in one respect: this time I'd brought gloves.

I closed the car door, turned the collar up on my jacket and took a look around. The road was dead. This wasn't a surprise. I doubted much traffic at all came out this way, especially at night. Besides the cemetery, which no one reportedly dropped in on anymore, there wasn't anything out this way that would have people itching to make a visit this time of night. Only a handful of farms and their large fields resided out here, and the next town was over twenty miles away.

I watched my breath turn to mist and drift off into the night before turning my attention back to the eight-foot gate. What I saw stopped me dead in my tracks, made my breath catch in my throat. To my astonishment, the gate stood open about ten or twelve inches, just enough for a body to slip through. The gate had been locked the time before, and I'd had no expectations that it wouldn't be this time. It was as if an invitation had been extended. From whom, I couldn't know for sure, but, I had an idea.

Like I was about to dive into a pool of water, I sucked in a breath and pushed the gate open further. The awful creaking sound emanating from its hinges made me cringe. If there was anyone else out there at all, either inside the cemetery or out, I'd announced my arrival.

Shhh, I told myself. *You'll wake the dead.*

I let out a slight chuckle, reminding myself that if I didn't hold it together tonight, no one was going to do it for me. I was very much on my own and felt every bit of it. I stepped through the threshold of the gate and into the cemetery.

For a minute or two, I did nothing but stand there and listen. A chill was the only thing in the air that night. There was no sound beyond a rustling leaf here and there. The breeze that tossed them was also very light and hardly noticeable. Everything about the cemetery was different from how I'd left it last time. Absent was the torrential downpour of tree limbs. And if there was agitation or a violent energy in the air, I didn't feel it. I dared a few steps further.

I moved gingerly at first, like an unsure toddler. Knowing I had to confront this situation or risk it hanging like a dark cloud over my life, and knowing how to go about it were two very different things. Between this and my encounter with Nick at Cue Balls, I was quickly becoming the master of the un-thought out plan. What was I supposed to do anyway? Beg forgiveness from a ghost? Without realizing it, that's exactly what I'd gone there to do. Not because I wanted to. But because I had to. I had to convince Connor that leaving him behind was a mistake. One that I regretted and was truly sorry for. But, a mistake nonetheless, and one for which I was indeed seeking forgiveness.

The cemetery wasn't like a lot of others where narrow roads weaved through the rows of graves, neatly dividing it into sections. There were no roads here, or even paths for that matter.

Just a sea of grass and slanted granite, trees scattered here and there. Clumps of weed-strewn shrubs grew anywhere they could find space, often spreading beyond their original confines. This was an old cemetery, thrown together without much planning or forethought. Very much like my actions of late. So with no direction or reason to lead my way, I simply started walking up the middle, cutting the cemetery in half. It seemed as good a plan as any.

To my left, there was a small rise. I pictured throngs of zombies coming stiff-legged over the hill, arms perpetually outstretched in a sort of dead, but not dead march. Staggering and slumped, the way George Romero showed us. *They're coming to get you, Barbara.* A shiver ran through me. I pulled out my cell phone, turned on the flashlight app and continued on.

The more graves I ventured passed the more my apprehension slowly began to release its grip. The tight muscles running from the base of my neck to my shoulders experienced a slight amount of liberation. I guess I had expected a display like I'd gotten last time and had prepared myself for it. Instead, I was being greeted with a quiet, calm cemetery. Emphasis on calm. Even the fallen leaves rested, having long since given in to their fate. I kicked a stick and watched it tumble along the hardening ground. Soon everything around me would be covered with snow.

It was the lack of anything happening that eventually became unsettling. Last time, all hell had broken loose by now, and a million reasons why it wasn't this time were running through my mind. Could the other night have been a fluke? A storm, after all? Perhaps my mind had simply imagined it all, thanks to a couple of light beers that may have had more of an affect than I would have thought. Or, and this was my hope and best case scenario, maybe the whole ordeal was simply over. Maybe, now, with

Nick's death, the ghost or spirit or whatever it was finally rested, its thirst for revenge sated.

Or, quite frankly, maybe I was just being fucked with.

"Connor!" The second the name arose from my throat, I regretted shattering the silence. It had come out louder than I'd intended, and I wished I could take it back as the muscles in my neck and shoulders once again tensed. The hair at the base of my scalp bristled as I waited for something to happen, expected it even.

But, nothing did. The cemetery and the surrounding air remained as calm and peaceful as it had a moment before. Still, the damage had been done. Paranoia became my guide through the darkness as I sensed invisible walls closing in. Shining my light up into the trees, their bare limbs reached for the sky like skeleton arms stripped of all flesh. Only the ribbons of moonlight cutting through the overhead branches kept the cemetery from feeling like one large tomb.

I wasn't sure I'd heard it at first. Tilting my head, I strained to hear it again. That is, if I'd heard anything at all. Was my mind playing tricks on me; cruel, unsympathetic tricks?

But then it came again, and this time, there was no doubt. Drifting through the night air, the faint giggling of a child. I was instantly reminded of Connor's inability to remain silent during our games of hide and seek.

I scanned my light all around, trying to determine from where the soft sounds had come. A slight breeze kicked up, making it more difficult to hear above the sudden rustling of churning leaves. But I heard it nonetheless. The giggling. A little louder this time, as if being mindful of the rustling leaves, intent on being heard. It sounded as though it came from deeper in the cemetery. Further back and off to the right, it was an area I either didn't remember or wasn't familiar with. Then I realized why.

The receiving vault lay in that direction.

Swallowing hard, I let the beam of light from my cell lead the way toward it. One step at a time. Left. Right. Left. Right. I pushed myself like a soldier on a grueling two-day march.

It was their beaks that first caught my attention. Perched like sentries atop the granite headstones were countless black birds. I hadn't noticed them before, but it was no fault of my own. Otherwise black as a shadow at midnight, only their long, sheeny beaks glimmered in the moonlight. Like tiny mirrors. There had to be thirty, forty of them total, all gathered in a tight group. All eyes on me.

The giggling came again, louder and more robust than ever. Practically full-on laughter at this point. The hollow echo that followed confirmed a fear that had taken root in the deepest reservoir of my stomach. I wasn't yet close enough to be sure, but my guess was the playful, child-like cackling wasn't just coming from the direction of the receiving vault. It was coming from *inside* the vault. That place where the dead were stored in the winter when the ground was too hard to dig. The place where no kid would venture during hide and seek.

And the place where Connor Westphal's body had been found.

With a deep breath of October air, I battled through the growing anxiety and took my first steps toward the giggling, and somewhere beyond, the vault. The birds' heads all turned slowly as I passed through their neighborhood, their eyes never turning away. They were alert to my presence, but somehow not *on* alert, and I can't say I felt threatened by them, either. They were only there to play witness, and genuinely seemed as curious about how all this was going to play out as I was.

By now, the breeze had whipped itself into a full-on gusting wind. The trees swayed, their naked limbs clattered against each other. The whispers of leaves took on the persona of a murmuring audience. There seemed to be an excitement brewing that I didn't quite share.

Then, suddenly, the vault lay before me.

Carved into the side of a small hill, the only thing that let you know the vault was even there was the stone façade around the entrance. The rest looked like a heaping mound of dirt. Creeping around to the front of the structure, I used my hands against the stone to help keep my balance. The chill of the damp granite cut through my gloves. In the sparse moonlight, I could see that the heavy steel door was missing. All that remained of the entryway now was the rusted and crippled metal frame and a gaping black hole just wide enough to drive a compact car through.

As I leaned against the façade, my heart rate matched that of a mongoose facing a cobra, and for the first time, I wondered if I even had the nerve to peek inside; to actually find out if something or someone was indeed in there. It was while I debated this that the laughter came again. Lasting all of three seconds, it was enough to tell there was something slightly different about the laughter this time. It was less giddy. Less childlike.

And so very close.

I imagined less scary possibilities of what might await me inside than a vengeful ghost. Perhaps teenagers were using the vault as a motel room; a homeless man looking to disappear from society and stay warm while doing so. But, it didn't sound like there were more than one person, and what did the homeless have to laugh about anyway.

No, it sounded like a child.

The hair was the first thing I noticed when the light from my cell illuminated the inside of the vault. Dark hair. Not quite black, but a very dark brown. Like Ben's hair, I thought briefly.

Like Connor's.

The boy looked to be a few years older than Ben, sitting with his back against the mold-covered rear wall. His knees were drawn up to his chest. His clothes, at least what remained of them, hung loose on his cadaverous frame, his torn shirt revealing a knobby shoulder. Lifting his head, he looked at me as I stepped inside the vault. Looked at me and smiled. When he pushed his crooked glasses up the bridge of his nose, I recognized him at once.

Connor.

The light from my cellphone expired, plunging me into a world shrouded in black. I ran my thumb along the side of the phone, desperately trying to bring the screen back to life so I could initiate the app once more. My eyes strained, tried to adjust to the sudden loss of light, but it was simply too dark to see anything. I found my hearing worked just fine, though, as a shuffling sound reached my ears. After what felt like an eternity, I found the button, pushed it and lit up the room once more.

The boy, Connor, was on his feet, standing only inches from me.

I sucked in an abrupt breath and damn near dropped the phone.

"I knew you'd come back."

The voice was no longer that of an exuberant child, but a hardened young man who had already experienced a life's worth of pain, despite retaining the appearance of a twelve-year-old. The shiver that shook me was either from a rogue gust of cold wind, or the recognition that I had found what I had come here for.

Only now that I'd found him, I wasn't sure what to do. Terror careened through my body, reaching all my limbs at once. My feet wouldn't move, like they were being sucked into place by an invisible mud. I tried to voice a response, but the words wouldn't exit my throat. Eventually I was able to mutter a single word…

"Connor…"

But for Conner, my recognition of him was enough. His smile was a strange one, emphasized by the fact that Connor's face was caved in on one side. Smashed, like a rock had been used on it.

Yet he smiled. Somehow. "Adam. Welcome back."

The thing before me—Connor, ghost, *whatever it was*—reached up and put a hand on my shoulder.

"Everything's better now, Adam. You're gonna love it here. Nick does." The smile slowly faded from the ruined face, and Connor bit his lip. "Okay, he may not love it yet. But he will. Now that you're here, Adam. Nick will love it now."

The realization of what he was implying set in, turning my blood to slivers of ice in my veins. "Connor, I—" I took a step backward. "Connor, I can't stay here."

"Yes you can, Adam, and you will. You left me here once. All alone. That can't happen again."

My stomach churned like the wind that was now howling outside the door. It made a rushing sound, like air being blown across the top of a soda bottle. What stood before me, what spoke to me was a mere child, barely five feet tall. But his demeanor, and the perceived threat behind his words elevated my fear to an all new high. My hands trembled despite the warmth inside the gloves.

"Hide and seek," he continued, "isn't much fun by yourself."

"Connor," I said, taking another step back. "We called out to you. We did. We didn't want to leave you. But, we got scared.

We…" I had to stop myself before I started rambling. I needed to be concise and to the point, say the right thing. I had to speak the words I'd waited twenty-five years to say.

"Connor, I'm sorry."

Something in Connor's blank eyes flickered briefly. Was it happiness? Relief? Forgiveness even? He dropped his hand from my shoulder.

"Doesn't matter now," Connor said, the flicker having disappeared as quickly as it had materialized. "All that matters is that we're together again. This time forever."

There was something about his eyes that held my attention, despite the threatening words flowing from his crooked mouth. I couldn't look away. I was desperate, holding onto the hope of seeing that flicker again. Of getting through to Connor. I'd apologized, but still needed his forgiveness if I was ever going to be rid of the guilt. Then, I thought of Nick and instantly, everything changed. I suddenly, and possibly for the first time, recognized the grave reality of the situation. Forget the guilt, I needed Connor's forgiveness if I wanted to get out of this cemetery alive.

"Connor," I started, raising my hands in front of me, "I want to talk about that night. I want—"

"Shh," he said, shaking his head. "There will be plenty of time for that. After."

I was close enough to the doorway now that I could feel the frigid wind on my back. Suddenly, a stray gust found its way inside, scattering the leaves that had gathered on the vault's dirt floor. The leaves started swirling in a tornadic fashion behind Connor, and it was enough to free me from my trance. I took another step away from the—*my God, what do I call it?*—and it was only when the wind wrapped itself around me that I realized

I'd retreated outside the confines of the dank vault.

That was also when Connor's face changed.

His eyes suddenly rolled up inside their sockets until only white showed. His jaw came unhinged, dropping away from his face as a bone-shattering shriek exited what was left of Connor's mouth. It was a familiar scream and I knew instantly where I'd heard it before.

Like a solitary creature, the flock of black birds rose from their perches, wings flapping loudly. As they ascended into the night, the shrieking continued, threatening to rip through my eardrums. I clamped my gloved hands over my ears to protect them the best I could and watched, mesmerized, as Connor ran his hands through his hair. Gripping two handfuls, he ripped two clumps free from his head with an unimaginable fury. Horror and disgust shot through my body, and I fought back the urge to vomit.

Instead, I did the most logical and instinctual thing I could have done in that situation.

I turned and ran.

Chapter Eighteen

He stood in the crumbling entryway of the vault he'd called home for all these years and watched his old friend run, tripping and stumbling through the cemetery. Just like the echo from his scream, the nostalgia he had originally felt for Adam Bishop's return was quickly fading. Anger replaced it, and its intensity grew as he realized that Adam wasn't here to be with him and Nick, but only to ease his own conscience. He could hardly believe it. Adam was planning to leave him behind a second time!

He'd understood why Nick had fought so hard. Been so determined to get free. Nick had always cared more about himself than anyone. But, Adam, he was certain, would be different. Adam was supposed to feel more. Be more regretful over what he'd done all those years ago. More willing to right his wrong.

But, he could see now that Adam regretted nothing, and that made him even angrier. Fueled his hatred. Bringing Nick into his world had been difficult to do. He'd felt some remorse and even a little empathy. Adam, on the other hand, was making it easy on him.

One...

Two...

Chapter Nineteen

The gate was closed. I could tell that much as the burning muscles in my legs carried me stumbling toward it. I was sure I'd left it open behind me, but now it was definitely closed. Slamming into it from a dead run, the rattle of iron echoed into the night. My breaths were shallow and quick. My chest ached. Stripping off the gloves and casting them to the ground, my fingers fumbled with the latch in the dark before a sudden realization hit me.

Not only was the gate closed, but it was locked as well.

I heard a sound like the snapping of a large stick, and spun around. My lungs heaved. I searched the darkness in all directions, frantically searching the darkest reaches. But, I saw nothing. And the sound never came again. My mind was seriously out of whack, and I couldn't rule out the possibility that it was playing tricks on me.

But even though I couldn't see it, I felt it. A presence. Someone or some thing watching me from the shadows. Watching and waiting. Waiting for what, I had no idea, and was wary of finding out. All I wanted to find was a way out of this cemetery. Thinking of Cheryl and Ben, a wave of loneliness washed over me.

But I wasn't alone.

"Connor." This time I kept my voice controlled. I was

running low on bravery at this point in the game. I couldn't help but snicker nervously. If only it *were* a game.

"Connor, are you out there?"

From behind a large pine tree, the boy stepped into the clearing. He stood a mere fifteen feet from me. My heart sank. I'd failed to gain any real ground, despite all my running. That knowledge added yet another layer to my terror. I braced myself for the onslaught of more laughter. That mischievous kind that only a child can pull off. All at once playful and dangerous. But when Connor opened his mouth next, laughter wasn't what came out, and there was nothing playful in his voice.

"Thirty-six...thirty-seven..."

A shiver ran through me as, instantly, I realized what he was doing.

"Stop," I said, as calm and neutral as I could. "Let's talk."

This did nothing to dissuade him. The boy who used to be Connor, who used to be my friend. Connor looked me straight in the eye and kept on counting, like talking was the furthest thing from his mind.

"Forty..."

"Stop!" I yelled, this time making sure I was heard. The wind was ferocious now, and the gusts threatened any and all communication, even from a short distance. But that wasn't the only reason I was yelling. Fear had replaced all sensibility. "I mean it, Connor! Stop this now!"

But Connor simply stood there, counting like this was some sort of game. And that was the most unsettling part.

In the midst of it all, I sensed another presence. Briefly taking my eyes off Connor, I dared take a look. Cowering behind an impressively large headstone with a weeping angel on top was a familiar face: Nick Gant. But not the real Nick. Couldn't be. Just like this couldn't be the real Connor.

They were both dead.

But, they were here all the same. We were together again, the three of us, for the first time since we'd gathered so many years ago for the last time.

Suddenly, as if he could read my mind, the counting stopped. Connor turned from me, to Nick, then back to me again. His eyes narrowed and the left side of his face, the undamaged side, curled into a snarl. Then, in a motion so swift I wasn't sure how it even happened, he was face to face with me. Standing toe to toe. He'd covered fifteen feet without so much as a muscle twitch.

"Fifty-one…"

I spun and once again grabbed the iron bars as if the result would be different this time. Common sense told me it was futile, but I had to try. Nothing else about this ordeal made sense either, so why not hope for the irrational? Unfortunately, the gate was still closed. Still locked. I started to climb, desperation driving me upward.

Cold hands grabbed my ankles and pulled my feet free of their perch. I clung to the gate as the iron latch rattled against itself. Through the bars I saw my car, sitting in the gravel pull off only twenty yards away. Shimmering under the moonlight, it was so close, yet couldn't be any farther if I'd left it at home and walked to the cemetery.

My grip on the bars held fast. The wind whipped all around. My legs were being stretched out behind me, and the tug of war made my shoulders scream and my arms quiver under the strain. But I held firm with all that I had right up to the point when visions of how Nick's body had been found flooded my mind. The iron bars still clutched in a death grip, his arms torn clean at the shoulders. I shivered at the picture of my own future, and without thinking it through, made an improbable decision.

I let go of the bars.

My face was the first to hit the ground, as the staunch hold on my legs remained. Before I could even attempt to right myself, I felt my body being dragged backward through the dirt and dying grass, my chest and stomach taking the brunt. My face bumped along the ground even as I tried to keep it lifted, my hands scrambled for purchase, but continually came away empty handed. I heard a crack, felt a sharp pain and knew instantly that one of my teeth had been broken. An exposed tree root scraped along my ribs, and with a howl of pain, I regretted letting go of the gate. How could this possibly be a better option?

Then it all stopped. The dragging. The wind. Everything. It had all come to a halt so suddenly, it was almost as if none of it had ever happened. Though I was face down in the dirt with a raw abdomen and broken tooth, so I knew that it had.

I delicately rolled myself onto my back and sat up. I was alone and in a clearing about thirty feet from the gate. Everything was calm. Under different circumstances, I would have gone so far as to call it tranquil. But these weren't different circumstances. I knew where I was, I knew what was happening and I knew it wasn't over.

You're gonna suffer just like I did.

Connor didn't keep me waiting long.

"Sixty-nine!" The voice boomed from out of nowhere, as if from a loudspeaker. It was no longer the voice of a child, but someone much older. Someone more evil. Connor was nowhere in sight.

"It could have been any of us!" I shouted into the night, dampness welling in my eyes. Tears of anguish flowed freely. The ferociousness of Connor's voice had quickly turned my terror into something altogether horrifying. Desperation broke me. I clutched my ribs.

"Seventy-two…"

"We tried, Connor," I said, this time more soft spoken, less of a shout. "We tried to find you, I swear." I was pleading now in an attempt to be convincing. Which of us I was trying to convince, I wasn't quite sure. Maybe Connor. Maybe myself. Perhaps both. But somehow I knew my words no longer mattered.

"Seventy-four…"

As the tears ran down my face, I found myself blabbering. I was officially breaking down. All the guilt and sadness I thought I'd overcome in my youth had bubbled up and now flowed like a river. The weight of its exit was excruciating. My mind became so overwhelmed, I felt it barely hanging on. So this is how it feels to pay your dues?

"Seventy-six…"

I looked toward the tombstone where earlier I'd seen Nick. He was still there, though more concealed by the stone now. His head barely peeked out from behind the stone monument.

"Nick," I pleaded through the tears. "Nick, I'm sorry."

The only acknowledgment he'd heard me was to simply pull back and disappear behind the stone completely, his eyes cast downward. He was going to help me about as much as I was willing to help him before. Then I realized there may have been another reason he'd disappeared.

The boy was back. He stepped into my field of vision, now blurry from the tears. I looked up into his face and it was Connor this time. Regular old Connor. Not the emaciated creature with the smashed face. Not the otherworldly being capable of the booming voice. Just Connor. Beautiful as he was the last time I'd seen him twenty-five years ago. His familiar frail body and boyish face still innocent. Untouched by evil.

Seeing him this way slowed the flow of tears. I breathed in deep and slowly exhaled. My muscles started to relax as I sat there in the dirt. It was so good to see him that way. And hopefully, seeing him like that was a good sign. Hopefully, it meant that this whole ordeal was over.

The look on Connor's face, however, became difficult to read, and I had to caution the hope building inside me. His eyes were clear, but showed no emotion. There was no smile, no upturn of his mouth at all. He was just there, looking at me. After a moment, I couldn't take the waiting any longer.

"Connor?" I said, slowly rising to my feet. I was taking a chance getting up and didn't want to appear threatening.

But Connor barely reacted. He either didn't fear my actions, or worse, he didn't care. Even his voice was dull and matter of fact.

"Eighty-five…"

The air around me was closing in. I felt its embrace, like being wrapped in a blanket, and it was becoming difficult to breath. It wasn't a warm, comforting embrace, but one of confinement.

"Eighty-seven…"

The grip on my body grew tighter. A pounding sensation started inside my head. The pressure kept building, too constricting for me to even move. The vice-like compression on my head grew unbearable right before it crushed the sight from my eyes.

"I didn't want to die, either, Adam," I heard Connor say. "But, you get used to it. Death is all around us here. Death is your new home. Ninety-two…"

Both shoulders dislocated at the same time, folding my arms

across the front of my body. I could barely breathe now and with the little air I could muster, I screamed. Screamed in pain. Screamed with sorrow. Screamed for the end to be quick.

"Ninety-seven…"

I was fading fast, but still understood what it meant when my insides exploded under the pressure.

"Ninety-eight…"

When my ribs collapsed, the scream was all I had left. It stretched the muscles in my throat to the point of rupture.

"Ninety-nine…"

When it gave, my veins burst and the taste of blood was all I knew as the world, mine and every other, imploded within me.

Ten Years and Nine Months Later

"When did you learn to talk to Dad?" ten-year-old Elijah asked his older brother from the back seat.

"Probably around your age," Ben Bishop said. "Mom showed me."

"And now you're showing me." Elijah wore the grin of a child who knew he was being let in on a very big secret.

"That's right, Buddy. Mom and I think you're ready."

"Cool," Elijah said.

Ben looked up at his younger brother in the rearview mirror. He was a spitting image of their father with a little of their mother mixed in.

"Does anyone else know you can talk to Dad?"

"Nope." Ben said. "Only me and Mom, kiddo. And, now you. Remember, though, it's a secret. You can't tell anyone."

Elijah nodded, then returned to staring out the window.

The brothers rode in silence along Azalea Avenue, not saying a word until Ben pulled the car off the road and onto the tiny gravel parking lot in front of the old cemetery. After he'd shut the engine off, Ben sat back in his seat and looked up at his brother in the rearview mirror. The excited grin was gone, having been replaced by a look of concern. When Ben had first told him about getting to meet their father, Elijah had been excited. But now that they were here, the boy looked uncertain as he stared through the back window at the looming iron fence.

"You okay, Buddy?"

Elijah turned and met Ben's gaze in the mirror.

"Is it…" he started, then paused for a moment, biting his lip before continuing. "Is it scary talking to a ghost?"

Ben understood what was going through Elijah's mind all too well. He too had been afraid the first time. In fact, it had taken him a couple visits before he truly felt at ease talking to his father through the iron gate. Eventually, though, he'd gotten to the point where he'd ride his bike out to the cemetery a couple times a week. And for the last three years, he'd driven.

"I'll be right there with you," Ben said, as assuring as possible. "It's okay to be a little scared, but really there's nothing to be afraid of. We can't go in, and he can't come out. Those are the rules. Besides, he'd never do anything to hurt you."

The worry clouding Elijah's face seemed to dissipate a little.

Ben gave him a smile. "Come on," he said, unfastening his seatbelt. "It's time to meet Dad."

The air was warm, but it wouldn't be for long. It was late summer, and in Minnesota, winter came early. His mother talked on occasion about moving somewhere warmer, but the nineteen-year-old Ben knew he'd never leave Broken Tree. He closed the car door, leaving the air conditioning behind, and waited for Elijah. When he appeared around the front of the car, Ben took his hand. Together, they walked across the parking lot, which was no longer gravel but a mass of overgrown weeds and ambitious grass, and approached the eight-foot tall entrance.

The iron gate had remained locked since the day after his father died. At some point, a chain and padlock had been added, but he wasn't sure when exactly. It had been there, snaked through the bars and rusting in the elements for as long as he could remember. There was no doubt the keys had been tossed in the trash, like all things that would never be of use again.

Three deaths in twenty-five years, the last two unexplained, had generated enough fear in the small town that people generally stayed away. Other than the legend of the three ghosts, or one of the alternate versions that occasionally reared its head on school playgrounds and the hallowed halls of the corner bars, the old cemetery on Route 36 was all but forgotten by the people of Broken Tree. No one had been buried there since the death of Adam Bishop and anyone whose loved ones were already buried there simply had to let go of the idea of visiting them.

Standing before the gate, hand in hand, Ben looked down at his brother.

"Ready?"

Elijah nodded, and squeezed Ben's hand a little bit tighter.

Ben smiled, then offered a wink. Turning back to the gate, he wrapped his other hand around one of the iron bars. It felt cold in his hand despite the August heat.

\#   \#   \#